Space Traipse:

Hold My Beer

Season One

Karina L. Fabian

Laser Cow Press

Rockledge, FL

Copyright © 2019 by **Karina L. Fabian**

All rights reserved. No part of this publication may be reproduced, distributed or transmitted in any form or by any means, without prior written permission.

Karina Fabian
Rockledge, FL
www.fabianspace.com

Publisher's Note: This is a work of fiction. Names, characters, places, and incidents are a product of the author's imagination. Locales and public names are sometimes used for atmospheric purposes. Any resemblance to actual people, living or dead, or to businesses, companies, events, institutions, or locales is completely coincidental.

Book Layout © 2017 BookDesignTemplates.com

Space Traipse: Hold My Beer, Book 1/ Karina Fabian. — 1st ed.
ISBN 978-1-7334471-0-2

To my dad for giving me a love of puns and Star Trek. Love you!

Space: It's huge! You think Texas has big skies? Ain't nothing compared to the view out the viewscreens. And it's just full of wild places and interesting peoples. These are the adventures of the HMB Impulsive. Its mission: to explore those new and interesting worlds (wilder the better!), to seek out new peoples, and to boldly do what no one else has the guts to do! Don't believe me? Hold my beer!

Contents

Best Laid Plans of Vegetation and Cybernetic Beings..5

Polarity Panic 73

Foot in the Door 89

Day in the Life...139

Rest Stop 169

Best Laid Plans of Vegetation and Cybernetic Beings

Captain's Log, Intergalactic Date 676767.67 and how cool is that?

The Union Fleet has redeployed to Sector 7 in order to confront another incursion by the Cybers. Meanwhile, HuFleet has been left behind to patrol the other sectors and take up the slack. Frankly, I'd rather we be there in the thick of things, but after the unfortunate incident with the Cognitives, we're not invited. I guess it was worth it; we won the battle, and seeing an emotionless species worked into a frothing frenzy is a memory I'll treasure forever.

At any rate, the Impulsive has been assigned a diplomatic mission. We'll be hosting the engagement ritual of the Clichan prince to a princess of Kandor. Although the same species, the two worlds have been at odds for some time, and it's hoped an arranged marriage between the children of their leaders will bring peace and stability to the area. As an amateur xenologist, I'm especially interested in the courtship ritual, which must be carried out on neutral ground.

Captain Jeb Tiberius shrugged his shoulders inside his dress uniform, trying to coax the fabric to loosen up. The replicator had overstarched it again. Ah, well, it was only for a few minutes. Once he greeted the prince and passed him off to Lieutenant Loreli, he could make a quick change before the meeting with Security. Loreli, of course, looked perfectly comfortable, not to mention perfectly perfect, in her green, skin tight outfit, despite the stays and the 5-inch heeled boots. Once again, he admired her training and was glad he didn't have to do it.

The velour material played well even with the utilitarian lighting of the ship, with shadows and highlights that accentuated her curves and complemented the smooth bark of her skin and the aloe-shaped leaves that adorned her head where humans would have hair. Ever since they'd rescued her from that greenhouse and released her from the confines of her pot, the Botanical had thrived.

Loreli watched the teleporter pad, aware of his scrutiny but feigning obliviousness. Such training!

Behind the teleporter console, Crewman Dour tapped buttons. "The Clichans report ready to meet their fate," he said.

"By all means, zap them over."

A shimmer and a tinkling like the excited jabbering of the fairy folk of Midsummers Nine, and two figures appeared on the dais. Prince Petru dressed in the torn finery in the aquamarine that indicated royalty of his planet — frayed long-sleeved shirt held by a patchwork vest, his pants equally unraveled at the bottom and bearing parallel slashes from mid-calf to mid-thigh. Edor, his advisor, wore drabber shades of blue and his material was intact. They patted themselves, as if ensuring everything had transported in place. From the console, Dour nodded approval.

Jeb stepped forward, hand outstretched. "Gentlemen, welcome to the Impulsive. I'm Captain Jeb Tiberius."

The prince grabbed his hand and shook it in both of his. "Petru, Crown Prince of Clicha. Your device is extraordinary! When do we get one?"

"That would not be up to me, Your Highness, but I could put in a word with the Union if you'd like."

Edor stepped off the dais with considerably less enthusiasm than his sovereign. He said, "Please forgive the prince's indiscretion, Captain. He can be..."

Space Traipse: Hold My Beer, Season 1 ⚓ 7

"Impulsive? That's how we like 'em on this ship. Of course, we have a saying, 'Your right to swing your fist ends where my nose begins,' so please keep it in mind, and we'll get along just fine. May I introduce you to our xenologist, Lieutenant Loreli? She'll be handling the arrangements for your courtship ceremony with Princess Katrin."

"What are you?" the prince asked. His voice held awe and admiration.

Loreli quirked a smile. "A xenologist, as the captain said. But my species is known in the Union as the Botanicals. We are plant-based life-forms as opposed to meat-based like yourself."

"Loreli will escort you to the VR deck where you can pick the scenario for your meeting and courting your true-love-to-be," the captain said. "If you'll excuse me, I've got a meeting with our security officer and chief engineer."

"Is something wrong?" Edor asked. "We've heard reports that the Cybers…"

"No need to worry. They're halfway across the galaxy, and the Union forces are on the way to take care of them. No, this is ship's business. I'll see you at the reception. Lieutenant? Gentleman?"

At the captain's outstretched arm, Loreli led them out.

From behind his console, Dour muttered, "You're welcome, really."

***

The lazivator doors opened to the bridge, but Jeb paused a minute before entering to admire the view and give the reader a chance to visualize the setting. Like most iGotThis class vessels, the bridge was a small compact bubble with a 360-degree view of the space through which it traveled. Of course, the view was digitally generated; the bridge itself nestled securely in the center of the saucer section under multiple deck plates and shields. Most species thought the design overkill...until they met the kind of crew that generally gravitated to HuFleet.

Let's meet a few of them now.

To the right, in a horseshoe-shaped console that manned sensors, communications, and ship systems and could be tied to engineering and command functions by flipping the switches installed under the main console, Ensign Ellie Doall stood, fingers flying over the touchpad screens. Was she recalibrating the sensors? Scanning for potential threats? Tallying the latest ship's pool? Jeb never quite knew, though he guessed – and accurately – that she was doing more than one of those. Regardless, if he needed anything, he could count on her to already be on it by the time he asked.

On his left, in a similarly shaped console, Minion First Class Gel O'Tin stabbed one of his tendrils at the security board at a significantly slower pace than Doall. Probably following the progress of their new guests, or trying to, if the greyish blue of his gelatinous endoplasm was any indication. O'Tin didn't have a lot of experience with bridge duty yet. Not to mention the fact that the human interfaces baffled him easily. There were times when his technical incompetence exasperated Jeb, but there was no disputing the Globbal's talents in a fight. O'Tin absorbed punishment...then he absorbed his foes.

Almost dead across from Jeb, the helmsman, Tonio Francisco Cruz, lounged at his console, feet up on the edge while he told a story to First Officer Commander Phineas Smythe, who sat in one of two revolving chairs in the center of the room. Judging from how his hands were moving, Cruz was either relaying an atmospheric dogfight from his Union Air Force days or a fight he'd had with his grandmother. In the recessed alcove to his right, three extra crewman half-listened while they played cards.

"Then she hit me – Bada-bam! Glancing shot to my port thrusters. I had to make an emergency landing in Dona Tortella's tomato fields. I stunk of marinara all summer. I'm a-telling you. You don't snitch my nona's tortellini or her hovercrafts!"

"Your grandmother was quite a woman," Commander Smythe remarked dryly. "I wonder. If we invited her aboard, could she break you of the habit of putting your feet on the nav console?"

"Sorry, sir," he said. "Orbit's just so boring. Put her in the right spot and stick her on autopilot. Doall could handle it from her console."

"I have," Doall answered. "Captain on the bridge, by the way – or at least in the lazivator."

Cruz's feet came down with a thump and Smythe spun the command chair to face the back. "Sir! Are our guests aboard safely?"

Captain Tiberius strode in, but paused just past the double-horseshoes of Security and Ops. "Well, Dolfrick would insist they died in route, of course, but they seem fine now. I left them in Loreli's capable hands. Are LaFuentes and Deary waiting for us in the briefing room?"

Smythe nodded. "There has been giggling, sir. I fear the worst."

"Well, we'd better get in there before they devise some creative new way to blow up this ship."

"Or someone else's."

Jeb shrugged. "Don't care so much about someone else's, as long as it's the right someone else. Cruz, why don't you come join us if you're so bored?"

Immediately, a relief crewman jumped up from the card table to take over the helm. Cruz and Smythe joined the captain, and they headed to the briefing room.

As Smythe said, there was giggling coming from the room, the maniacal giggling of creative minds in collaboration. On an engineering marvel or mischief? Probably both, and that suited the captain just fine. The greatest advances in human science came from someone saying, "What the hell? Let's give it a try," and he encouraged that attitude in all his crew.

Of course, as soon as the door opened, the giggling stopped and whatever 3D image they'd been looking at was wiped away with a sweep of LaFuentes' hand.

"I hope you gentlemen have something good," Captain Tiberius said as he took his seat.

"O, *vera*, Captain. You gonna love this!" LaFuentes half stood out of his seat in his excitement. "See, I was having this nightmare..."

"Nightmare?"

"Yeah, it was intense! I was back in the Hood and the zombies were coming and we were trying to get to the Union evac point, right? And we're all piling into my cousin's ZAT, you know, the Zombie Apocalypse Truck?"

"We're familiar," Smythe said, "The same kind of vehicle you like to take on away missions, the one that only recently crashed through two Halderan establishments, a herd of cattle and a small hill."

"I rescued our people from the Halderan, though, and those cattle spat corrosives."

"They certainly did as the ZAT's front blade threw them aside."

"*Exatamente*! Just like the zombies in my dream – getting knocked out of the way, that is."

"You really drove trucks on a spaceship?" Cruz asked.

"The UGS Hood* was a generation ship, man. It was bigger than that town your nona lived in – tomato fields and all. But you're missing the point. That blade is wikadas. So anyway, in my dream, we plowing through zombies and *mi abuela* is praying and *uno primo* is screaming but another's all 'Ten pins, man!' And then the zombies turn into Cybers, and we're in space. And then it hit me. We need a wikadas blade for the Impulsive."

"The Cybers are on the other side of the quadrant," Smythe said.

LaFuentes rolled his eyes. "Says Union Intel. You think they're going to concentrate on one spot? Sooner or later, we're going to run into a swarm. I want us to be ready."

"All right. How do we attach a blade to the hull of the Impulsive outside of a trip to dry dock?" Jeb asked.

At this point, Chief Engineer Angus Deary took the briefing. He activated the 3D image they'd been snickering over earlier. The Impulsive rotated over the table. Damn fine ship, Jeb thought as he again paused to admire this ship and give the reader a chance to see it from the outside.

The iGotThis class vessel had four warp engines — two for drive, two for reverse — flanking the wide flat operations section, known as Other One. The saucer section, so shaped because why the hell not?, housed command, primary Sickbay and main quarters. It, too, had independent warp, though those engines stayed dormant until the two sections separated. A thing of beauty, despite the dings and dents from too many years of flying through subspace phenomena without stopping in dry dock for a buff. Personality, Jeb liked to call it, but really, a visit to dry dock meant having outsiders' crawl all over his ship questioning every modification. That inevitably led to months of Deary yelling and a mountain of paperwork to fill out, justifying every harebrained alteration that saved their lives.

Alterations like LaFuentes and Deary were suggesting today.

Deary touched a button and the Impulsive was shrouded in a bubble representing its deflector shields.

"We don't need a physical blade. We alter the deflector shields and reshape it." To demonstrate, he reached out and "pinched" the shield in front of the ship with his fingers and pulled it away. The shield pulled into a cone.

LaFuentes tapped some buttons on the table and the Impulsive rammed an asteroid, shattering it into a dozen pieces.

"Or, if we're dealing with a cyberswarm…" Deary used both hands to manipulate the forward shield into a blade. This time, the simulation sliced through the swarm of Cyber ships, flinging some aside while shattering others with satisfying pyrotechnics.

"'Ten pins, man!' indeed," Smythe commented.

LaFuente's eyes were almost as bright as the explosions in the simulation. "Yeah! But what's even better is you're actually deflecting stuff. The only thing hitting anything dead-on is the blade itself, and if they're shooting at us, it's all at angles to the deflector. You know, glancing blows."

"Play that again, half speed," Jeb said. It was even funnier in slo-mo. "So, what will it take to outfit us with a wikadas blade?"

Deary shrugged. "Ach, we just need to reprogram the deflector controls. Might have to reroute power to make sure the points of contact are reinforced.

Permission to enable reroute to life support for extreme emergencies?"

"No problem. We have enough ambient heat and air for half an hour after they turn off. If we aren't out of the battle by then, we're probably goners anyway."

"So we can do the modification?" LaFuentes asked. "Like, now?"

"We have an easy cruise to Kandor. Engineering should have the time. Beer me."

"Yes!" The security chief and chief engineer high-fived.

Jeb tapped the console and his ship with its wikadas blade plowed through a cyberswarm battle. The enemy's shots glanced off the reshaped shields while the ship zig-zagged through the swarm like a ZAT though a zombie hoard. Pow! Boom! Splat!

He loved his job.

***

Loreli stood at the control panel and scrolled through the virtual reality deck settings. The diplomatic offices of both planets had given her several suggested environments in which to place the royal courtship and multiple scenarios, romantic and otherwise, where the prince and princess could meet, conflict, and eventually reconcile.

It was a fascinating twist on humanoid mating. Many of the scenarios the Clichans provided would have easily made plots for human romances, particularly the kind Ellie called "romcoms," but Loreli's observations had shown her that most human relationships began with friendship and attraction. The Hierarchy chose mates based on complementary support, rather than conflict. The Bonks were all about conflict, but they were straight up about it. Only the Clichans had codified it to such ritual: meeting, judgement, inciting incident, conflict, mutual appreciation, resolution, love & matrimony.

This was going to make a great presentation for the Xenologists' Symposium next year.

If she ever got to see the ritual through to completion. In less than 30 minutes, Prince Petru had declared every suggestion unsuitable for the most important romance of his life.

The heir apparent paced the length of the VR room, expressing his emotion through motion, as most fauna species did. He didn't have a lot of space for pacing; the room was set for "Space Pirate and His Captive" and the captain's ready room was crowded with treasures, beautiful jewelry on display and a large wardrobe of women's gowns. Petru himself was dressed in the full regalia of an Alurian captain – or the VR equivalent. In reality, he wore a Greensuit, a simple jumper made of material that accepted the computer's commands to create the image of any number of costumes. Once they had settled on a scenario, Loreli would have the appropriate garments made.

Petru would have looked quite dashing and romantic, if he didn't pace half-hunched over and if he'd stop slapping at his plated hair with the palms of his hands. Just exiting adolescence, he had the wiry physique that often came with youth. He also had a pimple, carefully camouflaged but not invisible.

Was that why he was nervous? Many species considered acne attractive, a symbol of youth, indulgence and hormonal excess, but the Clichans, like humans, found them embarrassing. She made a note to take him to Sickbay. The doctor could clear it up with a simple ointment and a pituitary suppressor.

"You are being ridiculous," Councilor Edor argued. For a diplomat he had little patience for his prince. "Are you sure you don't like the classroom rivalry scenario? That's how my wife and I fell in love, and we are still together after 40 years. It's a classic."

"This isn't just any budding romance," Petru said. "We are uniting worlds for the first time since the Breakup of 3221. The place of our meeting has to be big, with high stakes, high emotion, serious consequences if we don't put aside our differences and see the best parts of each other."

"The union between our worlds is already high stakes!"

"You don't understand me!" the prince cried. "You can't understand what I'm dealing with. Now get out."

"Prince Petru..."

"Out! I am the prince, and this is my courtship, and you are not helping. Now get out!"

Edor threw his hands in the air and spun away to leave. He paused and heaved a huge sigh. "Where's the exit?"

Loreli opened the door. "If you take a right, three doors down, you will find the mess hall. I will alert Commander Smythe that you are there. Perhaps he can arrange a tour of the ship while the prince and I continue our work here."

Edor's angry expression softened. He bowed, keeping his eyes on her, which in that position, meant her chest. Apparently, 40 years of marriage didn't mean he didn't appreciate other females. Not that Loreli minded, of course. Part of her job was to be appreciated, and as a botanically-based life form, it was her nature to thrive on being admired.

"You are as gracious as you are beautiful," he said.

"Thank you. Take a right, then third door on the right."

When Edor had left, the prince flopped into the captain's chair and set his booted feet on the desk. He would have looked quite charismatic except that he whined, "I don't want to get married!"

"Oh? Would you care to elaborate?"

"I'm only 22. I haven't even had my first kiss yet...unless you count the serving girl, but she was egged on by my mother and it wasn't true love...and actually, it was kind of gross. She had bad breath and her hands smelled like floor cleaner. But the point is, I haven't had a chance to live! I don't want to be stuck with the same person for the next 120 or 130 years."

"Perhaps Princess Katrin will die a young and tragic death," Loreli suggested.

"Well, yeah. One can hope. I mean, the grieving widower, determined to do well by his wife's people? I could do that! Plus, sympathy attraction? I have heard the stories! Wow. Is, is that true for other species?"

"Sympathy generally inspires maternal feelings, though I have heard of a phenomenon called 'pity date.' It is generally considered a bad thing."

"Well...what about you? I mean, your species?"

"We don't 'pity date.'"

He dropped his feet to the floor with a *thunk* and approached her. "No, I mean...how do you...? It's just, Botanicals are plants, right? But you look so, so..."

"Botanicals reproduce through several means. I spore once every five of Botan's years. At that time, I will return to my homeworld, take root, and wait for the summer winds."

"'Summer winds.' That's romantic," he murmured. He took a step closer.

"As for this form, when I decided to join the HuFleet, I chose it to better fit in with my crewmates. It's simply a matter of proper pruning. My natural form is far less curvy."

"I'd like to see your real form. I'll bet you're even more beautiful."

His face had turned pink, making his zits stand out even with the concealer. It was kind of adorable, like a bud waiting to bloom. She made a note for her report. However, the hopeful look in his eyes put her on Yellow Alert.

He was young; a cold shoulder should deflate his attraction and perhaps make him more cooperative in planning his coming romance. She turned away coolly and started scrolling through files. "That would not be possible until my retirement. What about Hostiles in the Hood? Cyberzombies overwhelm Level Seven and two rival gangs band together to fight them off. Lieutenant LaFuentes uses it to train his team on leadership and wartime diplomacy, but if you and Princess Katrin took the role of rival gang leaders... What are you doing?"

Petru had moved behind her and put his hands on her waist. "You're so pretty and you smell nice."

"Prince Petru, unhand me and back away." She froze and spoke as harshly as she dared.

"Come on. Be my forbidden affair! It doesn't even have to be love. You can forever be the smile on my face that my queen doesn't understand."

His hands tightened on her and he pressed closer.

"I'm warning you one last time. Back off now, and we can forget this."

He rubbed his cheeks against the thick leaves that passed for her hair. "Aren't you feeling the summer wind now?" he murmured. One hand gripped the fabric of her outfit while the other blocked her escape.

"Security to the VR room. Petru, stop that before—"

Suddenly, the prince screamed and jerked away from her. He clawed at his face where a dozen small needles pierced his skin. He passed out.

She managed to catch him and lower him to the ground just as security ran into the room.

"Oh, harvest." She sighed.

***

Captain Tiberius and Chief of Security LaFuentes arrived in Sickbay at the same time, a good thing, because Commander Smythe and Minion O'Tin were having a hard time containing the irate Clichan councilman. Or rather, Smythe was having a hard time. O'Tin had offered to contain Edor quite literally by enveloping him in his gelatinous body, and Smythe had sent him to where Loreli was sitting with her hands clasped to get her statement. Meanwhile Smythe stood between them and Edor, speaking with stoic calm while the councilman yelled and gesticulated behind him to the bed where the doctor worked on the injured prince. At the moment, that mostly consisted of passing a tricorder over the prince's moaning form and reassuring him and his guardian that he was not in any danger.

LaFuentes broke off to talk to Loreli while the captain approached his first officer, arms spread, voice loud. "Well, now, what's all this ruckus?"

"What kind of circus are you running here, Captain?" Edor demanded. "First, I'm sent away from the planning, then your, your, plant person attacks the crown prince of Clicha! Is this a Union conspiracy to keep our worlds divided and weak?"

"That's a load of crap, Captain!" Gel hollered from where he stood beside the xenologist. "Their rockheaded prince ordered him out of the room so he could put the moves on our ship's sexy!"

"Language, Mr. O'Tin," Smythe scolded, glad that the universal translators chose to use the literal translation of the Globbal insult rather than a more insulting derivative.

"All right," the captain said. "How about we start with the important things? Doctor? The prince all right?"

"He will be," Doctor Guy Pasteur said. "He took 13 of Loreli's defensive needles to the face. They're naturally

Space Traipse: Hold My Beer, Season 1 🐝 23

tipped with capsaicin. Highly irritating under normal circumstances, but so many to the face... Let's just say he's learned a painful lesson about sticking his nose where it doesn't belong. He'll be all right. I've given him .2cc's imposazine and a pituitary suppressor. Bonus: It'll take care of his acne. He'll be clear-faced for his fiancé-to-be."

With that, Pasteur turned back to his patient, waving a pen-like instrument over his face, occasionally touching it to a particularly nasty pimple. Pasteur was average in height, with blond hair and brown eyes, good at his job but lacking the flamboyant personality of the rest of the crew. You know – the type that gets added because they think he'll be a stabilizing influence on the crew, but just gets killed off later because his character's too dull to compete?

(Foreshadowing? No, no foreshadowing here. Why would you ask that? Moving on....)

Having received the doctor's diagnosis without anything interesting to play off of, Jeb turned to Loreli. "So. How did he get a face full of prickles?"

"I'm sorry, Captain. It's an autonomic response. He was trying to bury his face in my fronds."

"Your...?"

"Eyes up, Captain."

"Oh! Your fronds! Uh... Why?"

"He had indeed ordered the Councilman out, but I don't believe he had any hostile intent. The prince was merely frustrated and feeling pressured by his impending courtship. He began to vent this frustration, and as I searched for a more unique setting for him and the princess, I asked questions. I merely intended it for research, but he seemed to think I was expressing some romantic interest. I tried to brush him off gently, but he got aggressive surprisingly fast."

"What surprise?" LaFuentes said. He jerked his head at the prince. "He's royalty, but he ain't in charge yet. That means he's young and entitled. I knew plenty like that on the Hood."

"Can you blame him?" the councilman countered. "Look at her. He's young, inexperienced and nervous. What is it you call her? Ship's sexy? How is any man supposed to resist her?"

Loreli glared at him with narrowed eyes, her fronds stiffening in anger. Gel and Enigo took steps back.

"Councilman, in the five years I have served aboard HuFleet ships, I have been around thousands of people who were attracted to me – people of multiple genders."

"Whoa? Really?" Gel asked. LaFuentes elbowed him, which made him jiggle like a hospital dessert.

Loreli continued. "As ship's sexy, it is my role to be desired, and I have been trained in how to handle it. I have been propositioned 792 times, and each one of them took 'No' for an answer. Until now. I did call security when things began to escalate, and I did warn him. As the doctor has said, he's learned a painful lesson."

"Well," the captain said. "Sounds like self-defense to me. The doctor will have him cleaned up by the time we get to Kandor, so I think we should just forget this happened."

"But—"

"Councilman," Commander Smythe said, "perhaps you have not had time to learn all the Union rules, but there are dire consequences for making unwanted physical contact with a ship's sexy. They are, as the tradition states, 'eye candy to keep up morale and ratings while serving as an invaluable member of the crew.'"

"It's true," Jeb agreed. "You don't mess with a ship's sexy."

"Especially ours," LaFuentes added, threat clear in his tone.

Edor sighed and raised his hands in the universal sign of surrender.

"There is still the problem of the ceremony. We never did come up with a scenario," Loreli said.

LaFuentes curled his lip. "How about we throw him in the brig and let his fiancé-to-be break him out?"

"Now, Enigo."

Loreli said, "Actually, Captain, it would make for a unique first meeting. It's worth mentioning to the prince."

"No!"

All heads turned to where the prince sat up in bed, hair disheveled, eyes wild, skin perfect.

"No! I will not have it! I have decided. I know exactly what I want."

"Praise the gods!" Edor said.

The prince pushed the doctor aside, who went mildly enough because, hey, not his problem. Prince Petru patted his hair into place, stood, threw back his shoulders, and strode to Loreli. Two manly steps later, he ran and fell kneeling before her. Before Enigo or Gel could react, he grabbed Loreli's hand and looked up into her eyes.

"Loreli! Oh, beautiful, beautiful Loreli. We've known each other for so little time, yet you've taught me so much about humanity. About being a man. I understand now! It's as if...as if my life was enshrouded in clouds and you, shining beacon, have burned away the fog. Oh, sweet Loreli, I cannot be without you."

"Loreli of the Impulsive, child of the Botanicals. I want you to be my wife!"

***

Captain's Log, Intergalactic Date, 676768.69, which is even more fun to say than 676767.67.

Prince Petru has apparently fallen in love with our xenologist and ship's sexy, Loreli. Not that anyone can blame him, but it's making it hard to complete our mission of marrying him off to the princess of his neighboring world and thus ensuring peace in the system. Not to mention the fact that he's become a nuisance. He will not take her "no" for an answer, and LaFuente's "stay the hell away from her" only seems to egg him on. For now, we've assigned Loreli a 24-hour security detail and are looking for alternatives to discourage the impetuous prince.

In the meantime, work has progressed on the wikadas shields, as Commander Deary and Lieutenant LaFuentes have dubbed them. They assure me we'll be ready to test them as soon as we get the prince hitched. I'm really hoping that means sooner than later.

Loreli checked her scanner, and reassured that no Clichans lurked the corridor ahead, started forward.

"Yo! Fronds!" LaFuente's voice called from behind her.

She allowed herself a smile that was half exasperation and half affection, then smoothed her features into the sexy pout she'd learned at the Academy and executed a turn similar to the one used by Galia Kay in last year's Top Model competition. Any other male on the ship would have at least paused a half moment mid-step, but Enigo strode toward her, frowning.

"Where's your detail?" he demanded when he was close enough to speak quietly.

"I sent Crewman Jenkins to get me some nitrate-infused hydrated soil from hydroponics. It's been a trying day."

"Nitrate? Going to do some heavy thinking?"

"You know me too well, Enigo."

"Yeah? What I don't know is why you are walking the corridors by yourself. You are perfectly content in your room."

"True, but I have duties."

"Which you can do in your quarters."

"Xenology, to be sure, but as ship's sexy, part of my job is to be seen and appreciated. It keeps ratings up."

He leaned against the wall and looked her up and down, but with a warm, familiar, affectionate way she soaked up like the sun. "You know, being able to protect you is good for morale, too."

"But that's limited to Security."

"Redshirts gotta have some perks. Human men get a kick out of protecting their women. We're hardwired that way."

She considered, and had to admit some truth to his statement. Even after millions of years of evolution, there was a primal drive to protect mates or potential mates.

"Now, come on. Allow me to escort you back to your quarters and get you safely rooted in your soil." He held out his elbow.

She sighed. "All right. Thank you."

"You want to thank me, plant one on me later."

"Enigo!"

Suddenly a voice called out, "Get away from my intended!"

Enigo barely suppressed a most primitive growl. Loreli patted his arm and stepped between them before he extended his primal drive to more violent forms of expression. "I'm not your intended. Petru, you need to put away this infatuation."

The prince grabbed her hand and kissed it sloppily, not the way she wanted to get watered, to be sure. "My beautiful Lorelee-root. I'm telling you this is not a childish whim. Why just now, I had Councilman Edor tell the Kandor that the courtship is off."

Enigo said, "Are you out of your mind? Your system's unstable."

"Katrin is unstable. She's already declared war on our planet — a war we will fight together as proof of our devotion."

Loreli jerked her hand away. "I have been very patient, Your Highness, but this has gone far enough. Go back to the councilman, have him contact the princess and beg her to take you back. I will not be the cause of war."

"But what of Helen of Troy, whose beauty caused one of your history's greatest wars?"

"Helen of Troy?" Enigo asked. He threw his eyes to the ceiling. "Pulsie, who's Helen of Troy?"

Dutifully, the computer gave a brief summary, which I'm sure the reading audience knows and I won't insult you to prove that I, too, can make an AI quote Wikipedia. Instead, let's focus on the fact that Enigo smacked his own forehead.

"She's not real."

Loreli added, "And I'm not from Earth. That is not my heritage. Your analogy completely fails."

"How can I fail if you are beside me?"

"That's it." Enigo took Loreli's arm. "I'm taking you back to your quarters where you can rest in a nice mud bath, and if you are smart, prince, you'll not be around when I get back."

"Unhand her!"

The prince swung at Enigo. He'd obviously had training. Another man might have found his jaw bruised. Enigo, however, was no ordinary man. With reflexes developed dodging rival gangs and zombies in the Hood, and honed with Academy training and the Power of Plot, the chief of security easily dodged the blow, grabbed the prince by the elbow and shoved him against the wall.

"I had one nerve left, crip, and you just stepped on it."

"Enigo, let him go before..."

"How dare you!" the prince shouted in dramatic, noble fashion. "You dare do violence to one of royal blood? You dare make a claim on my woman? Then you shall pay the price. Your Union will hear about – aaah!"

The prince crumpled to the ground, knocked out by the tranq patch Enigo placed on his neck.

Loreli groaned. "Enigo, you've made things worse."

He snorted. "Worse? I don't see how."

***

Captain's Log, Intergalactic Date, 676769.56.

Thanks to an altercation between our chief of security – who, for the record, was just doing his job, albeit a bit enthusiastically – and Prince Petru of Clicha, our peace mission has gotten more challenging than ever. Prince Petru has challenged Lieutenant LaFuentes to a duel for the palm of Lieutenant Loreli. No amount of diplomacy, scolding or simple horse sense can sway the infatuated prince from his obsession. I've brought together my senior officers and Councilman Edor to determine what to do next.

The iGotThis class vessels had three rooms that connected to the bridge: the captain's Ready Room, a briefing room and the all-species head. The head was currently occupied by Gel O'Tin, but that's probably TMI, so let's turn our attention to the briefing room, where Captain Tiberius, Doctor Pasteur, Lieutenant LaFuentes, Lieutenant Loreli, Ensign Doall, and Councilman Edor sat around a barbell-shaped table to discuss what they should do with a problem like Petru.

"I'm telling you, Boss, I can take him. Five minutes in the ring. I'll bring on the pain and fear." He cracked his knuckles, which indeed bore the tattoos PAIN and FEAR.

"We can't afford to humiliate the crown prince," Jeb said. He cast a look at Edor, who nodded agreement.

"This is a duel to the death," Edor said.

"And no one is dying or getting killed on my ship over a romcom, got it?"

"Yes, boss," LaFuentes said.

"And don't call me 'boss.'"

"Sorry, sir."

Space Traipse: Hold My Beer, Season 1   🍺   33

The doctor, however, asked, "But what if LaFuentes did die?"

LaFuentes laughed at the idea, the captain said, "Maybe you outta give yourself a hearing exam, Doctor."

Pasteur held up a hypo spray. "Just hear me out. Before the fight, I give him 40cc's imposazine in a delayed-reaction dose. Once it takes effect, it produces near-death comatose symptoms."

Edor paled. "Isn't that what you gave the prince for his acne?"

"No, that was .1cc. It's all about the size of the dose. However, Enigo, you're going to wake up with the best skin of your life. Provided, of course, you can bring on the pain and fear for about 10 minutes, and then throw the fight. Not that you'd actually have much choice as you'd be slipping into a coma. But can you make it look good? Then we just cart you off to Sickbay and pretend to put you in stasis. You can nap until we're out of the system."

"And Loreli?" Jeb asked. Doall, meanwhile, had started to toy with her hair. Readers will learn that this is a key indicator that she was working on an idea and had more than 30 seconds to implement it...or rather, readers would have learned that naturally if we hadn't just told you. She leaned over to whisper to Loreli while the doctor hemmed and hawed and finally suggested something about being too grief stricken to marry.

The councilman shook his head. "Prince Petru would not allow it. After winning a duel for True Love, he would feel doubly sure of the righteousness of his actions. Besides, no self-respecting Clichan would fight such a fight then throw away the prize. He'd lose face in the council and among his subjects."

Having gotten a nod from Loreli, Ellie interjected, "Captain, I think the doctor is still onto something. Forget the imposazine. LaFuentes, you throw the fight."

"But it's to the death!"

"I don't see how this helps, Doall," Jeb said, "but I trust your brain...and your impressive collection of romance novels. What are you thinking?"

Doall blushed to learn that her secret pleasure wasn't so secret. She'd thought she'd convinced everyone that the pad she carried everywhere contained only science journals and technical manuals. Nonetheless, she spoke with a voice that was confident and professional, because to do anything less would send feminazis screaming for the author's head (as if having a "ship's sexy" isn't going to do that, anyway.)

She said, "LaFuentes accepts the challenge. He gets to pick weapons, right?"

LaFuentes cracked his knuckles. "Phasers!"

"Oh, come on. You have to be flashier than that."

"Mech suits?"

Jeb said, "I'd pay to see that!"

Ellie groaned in frustration. "No! Knives, swords! Bladed weapons. Nice and flashy, with little tassels that do nothing but look cool and get in the way. Something that causes quick damage but not ugly bruises and can let you see the fear and desperation in your enemy's eyes before you strike a killing blow. This is about style. 'Phasers!'" She paused to snort derisively. "Anyway, we load the arena with bladed weapons. We bring in an audience – the crew, some of Petru's friends, and the most influential members of your society. The more happily married or lovelorn, the better, right? And Princes Katrin and her entourage.

"Enigo, you come in, fire in your eye, ready to fight – to kill! – to keep Loreli safe. The captain orders you to stand down, and you refuse. He threatens you with court martial, but you will do anything to protect the woman you love."

"Whoa, wait!" Enigo turned to the captain. "I swear, sir, we're just friends, really."

"Forget reality!" Doall cried passionately. "Petru doesn't care about reality. He's got this whole fantasy playing in his head, and if we want to win, we need to take his game and make it ours. So, if the captain accepts this plan, you have been secretly in love with

Loreli and are now taking the chance to not only come clean but to make her yours."

Enigo sighed. "Fine. But the Bloods and Crips gave up knife fights after the zombie virus hit. No one wants to get that up close and personal killing someone when he might already be dead. I'm out of practice."

Doall tsked. "Oh, is that too challenging? Suck it up. Besides, it'll make it easier to throw the fight."

"About that," the captain cut in. "I'm not sure I see the up side to this."

"I'm getting there, sir. This is good. Imagine the arena. The crew watches as their beloved security officer risks everything, from his profession to his life, for love. The Clichans, too, see his passion and sacrifice and can't help but be drawn in. Loreli watches from a corner of the field where she can be seen by both parties. Oh, and wear that pink tulle number you got when we went shopping on Visa. It makes you look delicate.

"The captain can't sway you, Enigo, and finally gives up. You face off against the upstart young prince. He gets a few jabs in but so do you. You don't gloat – this is too serious. This is love. You are fighting for the happiness of Loreli as well as your life. Loreli, you watch from the sidelines, wincing at each cut Enigo takes for you."

"Wait, I gotta get cut?"

"As Enigo spills his blood for you, the realization dawns. You love him! You always have but never knew until just that moment. And now, your happily ever after is at risk."

"I gotta get cut?"

Doall stood, knocking her chair over and making Edor squeak in surprise. "Suddenly, Petru disarms you! Loreli squeals your name! You try valiantly to defend yourself. You dive for the fallen blade, but it's just out of reach. You spin to find Petru hovering over you, sword raised. You glare at him with defiance even in your defeat. 'Do it!' you tell him. 'I would rather die than live without her.'"

"Whoa, *chica*! I don' got no death wish."

Doall ignored him but stood with her arms over her head as if clasping an invisible broadsword. "Petru pauses to say something charming and gracious about how he will care for her in your name, but what's this! Loreli has run onto the arena, her tulle skirts flying – we should set the environmental controls to cue a breeze. She throws herself over Enigo's body and raises her hand to Petru."

At this point, Doall kneeled in front of Edor one arm up as she pleaded, "Please, my prince. I beg you, mercy. Spare his life, and I will go with you."

Edor turned away, sniffling.

The captain cocked a brow in his direction. "Well, then. I still don't see how this helps get Loreli out of the marriage."

Spell broken, Doall cleared her throat and retrieved her chair. "Scenario One: Overcome by pity, Petru spares Enigo and presents Loreli to him for the sake of True Love. Katrin steps forward to take Petru. The audience is charmed, and mission accomplished.

"Scenario Two: Katrin intervenes on Loreli's behalf and talks Petru into letting the two lovers go.

"Scenario Three: Petru spares Enigo, but keeps Loreli. Loreli goes with him and does the heartsick routine until Petru releases her.

"Scenario Four: Petru spares Enigo, keeps Loreli and is deaf to her heartbreak. Edor, however, lets it slip to influential parties in both governments about how the bride despairs. On their wedding day, she approaches the altar, trying to put on a brave face for peace for the Union and knowing that the only way her True Love lives is because of her impulsive promise. Then – crash! The temple doors fly open! It's the human, LaFuentes! He rushes down the aisle and throws himself at Loreli's feet."

Again, Doall turned to Edor as she acted out the impassioned plea. "'Loreli, my love, my finest flower. I can't let you do this. I have no life without you. There are only empty days of torturous despair, knowing I

Space Traipse: Hold My Beer, Season 1 ❧ 39

have damned you to this loveless marriage. I will not be the reason for your sadness!' He turns to Petru. 'My Prince. If you must take my reason for living, then I insist – kill me! Now! I would have a quick death at your blade over the slow wasting away of my broken heart.'"

"Yes!" Edor sobbed openly. "Yes, this is perfect. Ensign Doall, you are a genius. This has to work."

"And if it doesn't?" Jeb asked.

The doctor shrugged. "I can give her a couple of pills of imposazine for right before the wedding. He can be an early widower, and we'll offer to take her body home. I can revive her when we're out of Clichan territory."

"So it's settled, then."

"It is not!" LaFuentes said. "I gotta get cut? How come I have to throw the fight? Why can't I beat the snot out of Petru and we let Katrin do the impassioned plea?"

Before anyone could answer Enigo's very valid question, the ship rocked and the red alerts started to sound.

***

Another blast rocked the Impulsive.

Captain Tiberius staggered and caught himself on a chair, muttering an apology to the crewman doing things that were important to the ship but not interesting enough to mention. Once again, Jeb vowed that he would make Deary upgrade those dagblasted inertial rattlers. They were designed to shake the ship when something impacted the shields, in order to bring a sense of urgency to a battle or emergency situation, but dang if they weren't inconvenient. He'd been asking for ages to have some kind of control on them, so people could get to battle stations without toppling. If his engineer could reverse polarity by 90 degrees, he could sure as hell handle a simple task like that.

Jeb braced himself and looked at the screen to see three Kandor battle cruisers.

From his safe and secure seat, Commander Smythe said, "It would seem the jilted bride has come to make her displeasure known."

At Security, Gel reported, "They fired once while we were hailing them, but shields were up, so no damage that time or this. Wikadas blade is not on line yet. I've got target locks on all ships."

"Good job, O'Tin! You're on the fast track for sure." Enigo held up his knuckles. Gel bumped them with his gooey pseudopod and headed to the minion bull pen to await another chance at minor glory on the bridge. The second-string ops officer joined without comment.

Doall's hands flew over her console. "Ready to hail Princess Katrin on the lead ship. Prince Petru is in the lazivator."

How does she do that? Jeb wondered for the hundredth time. He knew she didn't have a camera trained on the lazivator. He made Deary check on a regular basis. Too many people depended on that lift for a couple of minutes of "private time," a rare thing on a ship the size of the Impulsive.

He shook off his curiosity as the front viewscreen came alive. In the foreground paced an angry princess, while in the back a nervous but resigned captain shrugged an apology to Jeb.

"Princess Katrin, I presume? I'm Captain Jebediah Tiberius. How wonderfully convenient that you showed up. We were about to contact you. There's been a small mix-up we're hoping you can help us with." Jeb put on his most beguiling smile, the one normally used for people who hadn't already fired on his ship without warning.

The Princess Katrin did not return the favor. Her stunning face was only more impressive for her anger. She scowled with all the ridges on her forehead, and her flat-plaited hair seemed to tingle with energy.

"Where's the hussy?" she demanded.

"The...?"

"You heard me! The hussy who thinks she can sashay around the prince, using her alien wiles, and take what's rightfully mine!"

Loreli cleared her throat and stepped into view. "I believe you are referring to me. However, you are mistaken concerning the origin of Prince Petru's misguided infatuation. If we could just discuss this…"

"Shut up, you kingdom wrecker! Look at you! You're green, and I can't even imagine what's going on with your hair. What could Petru possibly see in a mealy-mouthed little skank like you?"

Jeb barely had time to register how impressed he was by the universal translator when Petru burst onto the bridge. "Pay no attention to that shrew, my fair flower!" he shouted. He hurried to Loreli's side, then pulled her close. He glared at the viewscreen. "Why are you here? I sent you a note."

Katrin rolled her eyes. "Wedding called off for TLA? We have a duty to our planets, and you're going to throw away peace in our time for that…that…"

"Her name is Loreli, soon to be Princess Loreli of Clicha."

"I don't want to be a princess. I don't want to be your wife," Loreli said again, her patience thinning. "Unhand me before I show the princess exactly what I can do with my hair. On you."

"You're adorable when you're angry." But he released her nonetheless.

Katrin said, "Oh? And you think I'm letting him keep mistresses? Skank! Captain, release this brazen minx to my custody so I can try her for treason and get on with my lawful courtship."

"I forbid it!" the prince thundered.

Katrin just raised one hand imperiously.

The Impulsive rocked as phasers from all three ships struck its shields.

"That took us down fifteen percent. Captain, let me fire back." Enigo said.

"Yes!" Petru cried. "Fight back! Fight for our love."

"Whoa. That is not what I meant!"

"Everybody, hold your horses!" Jeb ordered, trusting the universal translator to say something equivalent so he didn't need to explain the idiom. "I know you're frustrated..."

"Shut up!" both royalty yelled at him. Again, the Kandor ships fired.

"Shoot them!" Petru yelled at Enigo.

"I don't take orders from you!" Enigo yelled back.

Another shot, and Doall reported shields at 75 percent.

"But come on, boss!" Enigo begged.

"Katrin, if you'd calm down for just five minutes and let me talk, we can resolve this. I'm not here to start a war." Jeb said.

"Oh, there's going to be a war if you don't hand me over the wench."

"Now that's enough, young lady. Lieutenant Loreli is a respected member of my crew, and wenching is not in her duty description." A comm signal beeped on his chair. He gave Doall a quizzical look and she mouthed "Kandor captain." He grinned to himself. Had the Kandor captain called him or had Doall once again anticipated his needs? No matter. He sat down to see if he could have a calm, adult conversation with someone rational while the monarchs-to-be raged on.

"Besides, this isn't in your jurisdiction," Petru said, pointing to a side screen she could not see, but which showed the relative positions of all the ships on a star map. "You are in Clichan territory!"

"Yeah, right. The Kandors have claimed this land since the star famine of 2913."

"Ha! The Clichans have claimed it since Galandifax."

"What? Galandifax? Galandifax, who founded the first colony on Kandor? That claim transferred with him."

"No it didn't!"

"Yes, it did!"

"Uh, Captain?" Doall cut in quietly. Jeb held up one finger.

"You are as stubborn as your mother!" Petru yelled.

"And you are a fickle two-timer like your father!" Katrin yelled back.

"Leave my family out of this!"

"How can I, when they arranged this marriage, which you are throwing away on a vegetable!"

"Take that back!" the prince yelled.

"Captain?" Enigo said with more urgency.

"Actually, I am a vegetable." Loreli said.

Katrin sneered. "So glad we agree on something."

Petru stamped his foot. "Well I don't. Loreli is my true love and you have no jurisdiction. Captain, I order you to fire on those invaders!"

"No one is firing at anyone!" Jeb said.

"Can I fire at the Cybers when they're in range?" Enigo begged.

"The what?" everyone but Doall, Smythe and some needed-but-unmentioned first-string crew shouted.

The first screen split to show long range sensor scans, A Cyber hive had emerged from its transtellar gateway and was heading toward the system.

***

Captain's Log, Retrospective.

"Out of the frying pan and into the fire," as my grandma used to say. She was a horrible cook and hated replicators, but she had a lot of colorful metaphors. Usually while cooking.

Anyway, our original mission arranging the courtship of Prince Petru and Princess Katrin has rapidly turned into a war over disputed territory and the right of my ship's sexy to marry royalty. Which, to be clear, she has no interest in, but the Prince is adamant about rights and about having her. To make things worse, as I was trying to work things out with the Kandor captain, a Cyber hive entered the system through a transtellar gateway, and they aren't supposed to be anywhere near this quadrant.

"Red alert," Smythe called.

The lights flashed red and a shrill siren sounded, followed by a harsh male voice. "Get moving! This is no drill. We are in deep kimchi, so get your butts to your stations. Move! Move! Move!"

Jeb stood up and pushed Prince Petru aside. "Okay, playtime's over. Time to let the adults take over."

"How dare you patronize me," Katrin exclaimed.

Jeb smiled. "You're cute when you're riled. Captain, as soon as those Cybers recalibrate, they are going to be meaner than a nest of angry hornets. We'll cover you. Get the princess back to your planet."

"No," Katrin shouted. "You must save Petru. I demand you get him to safety."

"You're just full of demands, aren't you, young lady? Lucky for you, in this case, I agree."

She nodded. "We will cover your escape, then. Captain Courageous, to the fray!"

Behind her, Captain Courageous shut his eyes as if praying for patience.

Jeb shook his head. "I have a better idea. Why don't we give you the prince and you both get to safety? Captain to Chief Dour, teleport the Prince and his councilor to the Kandor ship."

"No." Dour said.

"'No'?"

"My mistress forbids it."

"Captain," Doall chimed in, "the Cybers have begun a telemetric sweep of the system. If we transport anything now, they could intercept and absorb the signal information."

"What was predicted has come to pass," Dour concluded.

Jeb sighed. "The old-fashioned way it is, Cruz, get Donner to prep a shuttle. LaFuentes, have security find Edor and get him on board. We're sending him and the prince to that ship."

"Not without my Loreli," the prince insisted.

"My duty is on this ship," she said from her console by Doall, where she monitored the behavior of the Cybers in hopes she would have insights to help them in or at least some really cool data to pass on in case of their deaths or integrations.

"Brave Loreli. This is why I love you. Then I will stay at your side."

"Incoming transmission from the Cybers, Captain," Doall reported. She put it on speaker for both ships to hear.

"We are the Cybers. We are many, yet one. We will integrate your uniqueness to our programming. Prepare for disintegration and reintegration. We are..."

"Blah, blah," the captain concluded and signaled for the transmission to be turned off. "Doall?"

Space Traipse: Hold My Beer, Season 1   49

"Cybers are almost done recalibrating to this system. Shields are up and holding, randomizer is running with three crewmen inserting changes at will. A complaint has been sent to Union Intelligence concerning their recent report on Cyber activity. And Minion First Class Ja'az in Environmental Science wins this week's crisis pool. Donner is in the shuttle bay and warming up the Killians."

"Excellent work. Ensign Gel, escort our guest to his escape. Cruz?"

"Donner's on the way, Captain."

"We don't have time!" Katrin exclaimed. "Don't worry about us. I have six sisters. Maybe one of them will better please the prince. Get him away and we shall defend you. Courageous, send the others to engage the hive."

That command, apparently, Courageous could get behind. He sent the two other ships dashing away to provide a diversion.

Katrin said, "Captain Tiberius, get your ship out of here. We'll cover your retreat."

Petru gaped at her. "You...you would sacrifice your people for me?"

In answer, one of the Kandor ships exploded under the Cyber's attack.

Petru flung his arm out of Gel's grasp. "Then we fight together! Captain Tiberius, I demand control of this ship."

Katrin set her hand on her chest. "You...would fight with me?"

"With you and for you – and always at your side! I am sorry, my Loreli, but my eyes have been opened."

Loreli gave him a gracious nod. Katrin squealed with joy and clasped her hands in a very dainty and un-warriorlike way. Doall clicked some buttons and 30 credits and miscellaneous chore vouchers went to Minion Martinez in Security for winning the ship pool on how the two royalty would finally fall in love.

Captain Tiberius, meanwhile, slapped his head. "Gel!"

Gel oozed his viscous body over the prince's arms and legs. Petru screamed.

"Quit whining. You could have walked out on your own," Gel said as he frog-marched the prince out like a puppet. Despite the warning, Petru kept shouting protests. He struggled so much that they left a trail of spatters. Immediately the Impulsive janitorial services dispatched a roving shop vac to suck up slime that dotted the floor and walls. It would later separate the bits of Gel and carry them to Sickbay to be put in stasis to reintegrate with the enthusiastic security minion later.

(Fun fact: Gel's species has fully adaptive DNA. Every molecule can be repurposed on the fly to take over some vital function. In fact, while this species does mate, they are perfectly capable of cloning themselves from even a tablespoon of their own fluid.)

(Fun Fact 2: It's going to pay the dedicated reader to pay attention to parenthetical comments.)

(Fun Fact 3: I'm planning on a long-running series. If you expect immediate payoff, grow accustomed to disappointment. And now, back to our story...)

When the lazivator doors shut on his last desperate cry, the crews on both ships breathed sighs of relief.

Jeb took a step toward the screen – or rather the teeny camera at the top of the screen that would note his authoritative move and focus on him instead of the closed lazivator door. "Now, young lady, you let us captains do our jobs, or I swear by my pretty flowered bonnet that I will send my security officer with the prince to escort you off that bridge."

Jeb didn't know for certain how the translators handled swearing by dainty headgear but whatever it used, it was effective. Katrin paled, then stepped back with a bowed head.

"Shuttle away," Cruz reported. "Moving to engage the Cybers."

"LaFuentes, when we're in range, fire at will – or better yet, the Cybers." Tiberius said.

52 ❈ Karina Fabian

Enigo chuckled. That joke never got old.

"Captain, the Cybers are targeting the princesses' ship!"

"Cruz, get us between them. Engineering. Deary, I need all power to the shields."

"Aye, Captain!"

"Into the jaws of death we go. Let's kick a hive!" Cruz said.

Doall sighed. "Metaphor mixing. Captain, they're firing!"

Before she finished speaking, the shields flashed bright, because, after all, light travels faster than sound or human reaction.

LaFuentes didn't even bother to announce his intentions. The captain said he could shoot; no one had to tell him twice. Among the pyrotechnic light show in the screen, they could see the Kandor ship moving toward the shuttle.

"Shields at sixty percent and holding," Doall announced. "About one in three of our blasts are getting through. Their shields can't adapt fast enough."

"You can't adapt to random," Jeb said.

"And we're as random as it gets," Enigo crowed. "Deary, give me one full power for one full spectrum shot and Dour, prepare a special delivery."

"My lady visits death upon our enemies," the teleporter chief intoned.

"Captain!" Doall shouted. "The shuttle!"

The Cyber ship had captured the shuttle in a tractor beam and was pulling it toward them. The Kandor ship fired but with little effect.

Enigo said, "Retargeting the tractor generator. Dour?"

"The hands of fate hover over instruments."

"Manos," Enigo breathed. "Firing!"

The entire ship dimmed as all the energies momentarily channeled into the phasers. Yes, even life support, because everyone could survive for a few seconds without the heaters on and the scrubbers going. It's a huge ship. The phaser banks didn't whine so much as roar as the power escaped. The Cyber hive's shield, vulnerable already at the point its beam passed through, flared with the impact. The tractor beam disengaged as the Cyber shields adapted, but the shot did not get through.

The shuttle rushed away, only to be caught again before it could get out of range.

LaFuentes swore.

Princess Katrin's image again showed up on a side screen. "Captain. Captain, what do we do?"

Jeb frowned. "Dour?"

"It is done."

He sighed. "Courageous, get your ships out of here and back to your planet. Get ready to defend yourselves."

"No!" Katrin cried. "Not without my Petru."

The shuttle disappeared inside the Cyber hive, the bay doors closing behind it.

Then that section of the Cyber hive exploded.

Katrin screamed and fell to her knees.

On the screen, a simulation of the ongoing battle still played. The princesses' ship held back but the Kandor ship renewed its attack, now focusing on the injured section of the Cyber hive. The Impulsive, too, continued to press its advantage, because the crew knew its job and didn't have to wait for the captain to tell them to keep doing it. That freed Captain Tiberius to handle the weakest participant in the fray: the princess.

"Courageous, get out of here — maximum warp!" he said.

Katrin stood. "No! We will engage the Cybers. We will break through their shields. We will board that ship and find the prince and rescue him!" Despite how hard she sobbed, she managed to spit out the words with fiery vengeance befitting a monarch-to-be who had just had her True Love snatched from her on the eve of her nuptials.

"Courageous?" Jeb pressed.

The captain ordered their retreat.

Space Traipse: Hold My Beer, Season 1 ✶ 55

"No!" Katrin ran to his chair and stabbed at the controls. "This is Princess Katrin, your future queen. You will disregard that cowardly order. You will attack the Cybers. You will save the prince!"

A voice from the back said, "But Katrin, I am already saved."

She looked up and gasped. "But... How...?" She turned to the viewscreen (or rather, the teeny camera that let her face been seen by the crew of the Impulsive.)

Jeb shrugged. "We don't question the teleporter chief or his methods."

Over the intercom, Dour said, "That is wise."

"Thank you! Captain Courageous, get us home."

The viewscreen went dark, but not before showing the princess run to the prince's embrace and their first kiss.

From Ops, Doall sighed.

Captain Tiberius shook his head, dismissing the alien teens from his mind. "Doall, status?"

She wiped a tear quickly and checked her console. "Shields at forty percent. Donner's safely in the shuttle bay. Edor made it to the Kandor ship as well. We were lucky we'd distracted the Cybers enough to transport them and put in that bomb."

"Teamwork, not luck," Smythe corrected.

"Yes, sir. Shields at thirty-eight percent. A couple of shots did get through. Teleporter crews are beaming in replacement hull pieces as needed."

The viewscreen flared.

"Shields at thirty percent."

Smythe said, "Mr. Cruz, we are no longer protecting the princess. If you could not fly into the shots now?"

"Deary, we need shields," Jeb said.

"Sair, you can't get blood from a turnip!"

"Tell that to the Russians. What about the Wikadas shields? Less power, more effect, you said."

"But we've not run tests... Ack! What am I saying? Ten minutes."

"You've got two."

"Then we're dead."

"Again?"

"An honor serving under you, Captain. *Dasvidaniya.* Oh, Danny boy..."

Jeb sighed. "Cruz, Doall, LaFuentes, buy us time."

"Debris field?" Doall highlighted the scattered remains of the destroyed Kandor ship on the screen.

"Hiding behind the dead bones of our fallen friends? *Tipo tosto*! Changing course. How about a distraction?"

"On it!" LaFuentes said, and a scatter volley of torpedoes left the Impulsive to impact against the already-injured side of the hive. But when the flares of impact cleared, they saw pieces of the hive pulling away of the core, each under its own power. They arched away from the hive, then started toward the Impulsive.

LaFuentes swore.

"They're swarming!" Doall said. "Transmitting jamming signal. On speaker, Captain?"

"Why not?"

A deep male voice came over the speakers, singing about searching for the perfect love.

The captain furrowed his brows. "Interesting choice."

"It was ranked Number One on Earth's twenty-first century's most played list, early teens."

"Oh?"

The voice went on about exclusive commitments.

"Top annoyance of the social media age. It should corrupt their systems."

Indeed, the Cyber ships had ceased their focused attack and buzzed about, disconcerted. As the singer launched into a repeated chorus about staying true, supportive and honest, two of the ships deliberately flew into each other.

Jeb nodded. "Nice. Catchy tune, too. Cruz, we there yet?"

"Parking us now, Captain." Cruz's hands, so wild in conversation, moved with Spartan efficiency as he slid the Impulsive between the largest pieces of the shattered Kandor vessel. Even so, a proximity alarm sounded.

"*Basta*, Pulsie! There's room for my nona's shuttle."

"All right," the captain soothed. "Let's turn off the lights."

Of course, the captain didn't mean only the lights, but rather anything that might broadcast their location. The music stopped, although a few people hummed the chorus. All outward lights shut off and nanites darkened the glass of the windows. Teleporter repairs halted. The deflector shields went off line, and the motherly voice of the Impulsive's main computer reminded everyone to stay away from damaged outer areas of the ship without radiation suits or anti-radiation vaccines. In Sickbay, Pasteur prepared to receive patients who didn't listen to their mother.

Tiberius returned to his seat and settled himself in comfortably. "Doall, keep an eye on those Cyber ships. Captain to Engineering. We bought you your time. Make the best of it. In the meantime, ladies and gentlemen, let's see if we can have a rip-roaring surprise lined up for when that new shield is ready."

***

Captain Tiberius leaned forward in his chair, concentrating on the viewscreen, which now showed the Impulsive in the center of a field of debris. With only the ship's passive detection systems operating in order to keep hidden from the Cyber ships, the locations were approximated by previous known locations and movement. Red blips showed the Cyber ships as they moved toward the wreckage, first a few, then more as other possible locations were dismissed.

"They're starting to poke around, Captain," Doall said as her console picked up the Cybers' active systems feeling out the field.

Jeb nodded. "Status?"

Smythe glanced at his console. "Wikadas shield online and formations programmed in."

"Weapons ready," LaFuentes said.

Doall added, "Jamming ready. I have a new selection: Classic Twentieth Century Metal. That should confuse them. They are entering the debris field."

"Cruz?"

"Just say when."

Captain Tiberius leaned back and pressed the intercom. "All hands, this is the captain. Time to make trouble. Mr. Smythe? Beer me."

"All hands. Silent Red." Smythe ordered. In response, the lights dimmed to red and brightened three times to signal the alert and for dramatic effect.

The power came on, all systems coming alive in a rush. The intercom blasted with a man's maniacal laughter. In the bullpen, the relief crew cheered.

The screen shifted to a completely accurate representation of the ships and debris locations just in time to register multiple explosions as Doall's musical choice caused some of the Cyber ships to veer into pieces of the Kandor ship.

As the guitar solo sounded, Smythe said, "Activating shield sequence one."

The deflector shields powered up in a programmed expansion that started close to the ship then pushed outward. Debris, mechanical and biological was shoved away from the Impulsive at high velocity and rammed into the approaching swarm. As the swarm jinked and dodged to avoid collision, LaFuentes and his weapons team followed up by blasting Cybers and debris alike to increase the confusion.

The singer began saying "Ai, Ai, Ai."

Smythe announced, "Wikadas blade formation two. Cruz, go."

The defector shield energies warped until they formed a blade with a horizontal edge that paralleled the width of the ship. The engines engaged and just as the singer began to sing of locomotion and insanity, the HMB Impulsive burst from its hiding place, plowing through debris and ships, phasers striking from every turret.

"Kill them all or make them run," Tiberius ordered.

The Impulsive swooped in and out of the fray, scattering space junk, ships, and ships that became space junk like a Fibaltian dragonhawk terrorizing a flock of hummingsparrows.

"Brace!" Cruz called as he entered the thickest part of the swarm. Across the ship people grabbed consoles or the arms of their chairs.

Just before they broke through the swarm, Cruz kicked the ship into reverse. (Heck, yeah, reverse! The Impulsive has reverse drive – impulse and warp. As Deary's father, Montgomery Angus Deary used to say, "U-turns in space are for people who don't understand engineering.")

The ship jerked with whiplash-inducing suddenness the inertial dampeners could not compensate for. The Impulsive cut back through the swarm.

Just like the alien bird mentioned earlier to remind you this is space opera, the ship twisted and dove through the smaller but plentiful enemy ships. Unlike the birds, the Impulsive and the Cybers fired phasers and launched torpedoes. The Cybers tried to form into a swarm for a coordinated attack, but as Deary and LaFuentes predicted, their best efforts bounded off the shields at angles, sometimes continuing on their new trajectories to hit their own ships. Doall reported the power drain, but it was a fraction of the damage they'd been sustaining earlier. LaFuentes whooped.

Jeb grinned, imagining the next time he was on Earth at the Captain's Conference. "Take that, Union Fleet."

The band on the intercom moved to another guitar solo. In the bullpen, the second-string team played air guitars.

"Captain! They're adapting," Doall announced.

On the screen, they saw the Cyber ships breaking away, retreating to a safer distance and gathering into a new formation, latching together like giant, evil, Cybernetic Space Legos. A few remained behind to provide cover for the retreat, and the Impulsive's weapons team made sure they paid a dear price for it. Even so, enough survived that they could complete their intended form.

As the new configuration started to become clear, Jeb swore. "Doall, jam them!"

"The jam is on all frequencies, sir – even FM. Kind of sounded better that way, too. But it's not working anymore. This must have been a programmed failsafe."

"See how they connect, then move?" Loreli added, because her job is to study alien behavior and because she hasn't been mentioned yet in this scene. "They're getting commands through physical contact. I've made a note for HuFleet and the Union tacticians."

The last of the Cyber ships broke off to join the rest, which had formed themselves into a large wedge.

"Bloody copycats," Smythe said.

"Captain?" Cruz asked. He'd slowed the ship and it hovered, ready to attack or run.

As if sensing his thoughts, Doall said, "The formation contains fifty-seven-point-eight percent of the original hive. Still enough to integrate the entire system. Our shields are holding at eighty-seven percent."

Jeb narrowed his eyes at the screen. The tiny camera by the viewscreen focused on his determined expression for its visual report and potential intraship memes.

"Smythe, sharpen that wikadas shield. It's chicken time."

***

Imagine, if you will, two ships hanging in the blackness of space. Alone. Silent. The crew waiting with bated breath for the commands of their captains. If warp drives could rev, they would.

Okay, now hold that emotional image in your hindbrain because it's good TV, but it's not really what's going on. In fact, on the Impulsive:

Smythe downloaded and encrypted the ships logs and deployed them by buoy and subspace transmissions.

LaFuentes was sending instructions to Deary, who shouted at his engineering crew, who scurried about making untested modifications for the battle while wondering if the chance to visit the pleasure planet of Alura was really worth the equally sized chance of dying a horrible death by warp core breach, panel explosion, or Cyber API.

Doall ran sensor sweeps and consulted with her team about new ways to disrupt the swarm's communications.

In the teleporter rooms, Dour's team was making sure the Einstein batteries were fully charged and typing in modifications. Dour downloaded his last pattern into Smythe's transmissions. If worst came to worst, he would return.

In the bullpen, the second-string bridge crew had put away their air guitars and were catching up on what the bridge crew was doing in case, you know, someone died and they got to step up.

Cruz was wondering how he could rev the warp drive.

Captain Jeb Tiberius was thinking about the last time he'd played chicken. It had not ended well. His father had grounded him for the entire summer.

On the Cybership, the drones were all thinking, "We are Cyber. We are integrated. We will kick this frickin' ship's butt, then integrate it." Of course, that's not a direct quote, but if the Impulsive were to voice it for the crew, that's about how it would come out, only Pulsie would not use the words "frickin'" or "butt."

Jeb asked his crew, "Got my miracle yet?"

"Not until we are in contact with the Cybers," Doall said.

"It's tricky and untested, but what the heck?" LaFuentes added.

"Show me."

Doall sent a simulation to the captain's console. He and Smythe grinned when they saw it. "That's imaginative. Cruz, ready?"

"*Dum vivimus vivamus*," he said, quoting one of the great space philosophers of his people.

Jeb gripped the arms of his chair.

Smythe raised a brow. "Your father isn't going to ground you," he said.

Jeb snorted. "Pa's an admiral. Want to bet? All hands, this is the captain. We're making history or dying. Saddle up. Cruz, redline those engines."

"Yes sir!"

In space, no one can hear you rev, but the impulse engines went from zero to full so fast that the astronomers on Clicha-Alpha-Two swore they saw the Impulsive buck and spring forward. Almost immediately, the Cybers reacted, racing toward them. At full impulse and then some, there was no time for anyone to have second thoughts or veer away. There was, however, just enough time for the Impulsive crew to enact their imaginative plan.

As the ship rushed toward the hive, the angle of the wikadas blade extended forward and rotated so it no longer met blade-for-blade. Meanwhile, the teleporter crews pulled from the Einstein batteries to convert the energy they contained into matter — pure unobtanium, the hardest substance in the known universe — into a very solid blade reinforced by the deflector shields.

The Cyber intelligence barely had time to register surprise when the blade sliced through its shields and the first row of ships.

"Initiating spin," Doall said, and the blade began to rotate, matter and energies bashing into the wedge-shaped hive from above and below and in between. When contact was made, the drones were treated to "Fibonacci Transforms in B-minor and C-major" by the Logic musician, B'Lather. Heralded by critics as "so complex and mind-numbing it may induce coma," the composition came with warnings for non-logic species. Of course, logic-based species often shunned the song because of its insidious earworm quality.

As communication between the Cyber ships shut down, replaced by the song, Loreli made a note to add Cybers to the list of alien races that should never be subjected to it. Or always. Can one adapt to an earworm?

Captain Tiberius frowned at the chaos on the screen as the Impulsive blended its way through the Cyber hive, which had become paralyzed beyond the ability to adapt or react.

"It's almost tragic," he said as Cruz swung the ship around to hit the hive from a new angle and LaFuentes took pot shots at the straggler ships. "Why hasn't someone used this before?"

"FTBC is forbidden on all human ships," Doall said. "We're just lucky we have a Logic on the crew that's a B'Lather fan."

"What? Ensign!"

"Don't worry, sir. We purged the ship's systems as soon as we transmitted, and Minion First Class Ja'az is in isolation until he can stop himself from humming."

"Sir," LaFuentes cut in, "I think we've destroyed or disabled the last of the ships."

"Really? That was easy. Anticlimactic, even."

"Captain! The swarm has activated a self-destruct—"

Before Doall could finish her sentence, the ship rocked as a handful of drones around them exploded. Immediately, red alert sounded. An engineering console sparked and electrocuted the crewman watching it. Immediately, three secondary crewman dashed out of the bullpen, two to drag their injured comrade to safety, one to assess the damage to the system and get it running. All three were too professional to yip with glee at the chance to be useful, but the two carrying the injured crewman to the lazivator did grin at each other when no one was looking.

Meanwhile, Doall reported aft shields down and damage to the engines. "That was the first explosion. The other ships were having problems concentrating through the song, but they've got it now. Next explosion in twenty…"

"Do we still have reverse engines? Cruz, get us out of here."

"I'm trying, but reverse will take us back into the swarm. Even turning us around will expose our vulnerable parts."

"Shields?"

"Shield control is offline. I can't remodulate," LaFuentes said.

"Engineering is on it, sir, but they had a feedback surge from the explosion that's wreaking havoc with the systems," Secondary Crewman #3 called from his still-smoking console. He barely suppressed a squeal of glee over having spoken a whole sentence in this scene. His name would be on the credits of this report for certain, now.

"Twelve…"

"Teleporters – Dour?"

"The Einstein batteries are depleted. It will be at least an hour before they can service my mistress again."

Space Traipse: Hold My Beer, Season 1 ⚛ 69

While Smythe made a note to – if they lived through this – once again counsel Dour on his phrasing, the captain called for evacuation of all outer decks.

"Nine – Captain. Four ships approaching. Seven…"

"What now?"

All eyes turned to the screen except for Doall's, who was concentrating on the countdown, and our secondary crewman who was composing a hasty message home to tell his mom about his big day. If it was his last alive, he wanted her to know he died relevant.

On the screen, two Kandor ships and three Clicha vessels warped into view. They immediately extended their shields around the Impulsive.

"One."

Wrapped in a cocoon of five shields, the Impulsive didn't even rock as the explosions sent shock waves through the system.

The crew cheered.

Princess Katrin's face appeared on the screen. "Impulsive, are you all right?"

Captain Tiberius laughed. "We've been better, but we'll live thanks to you. That was close."

Katrin sighed. "I wanted to be here earlier, but Petru insisted we wait." She looked offscreen with an exasperated but besotted smile. The viewscreen camera panned out to show Petru approach her side and take her hand. After giving her an adoring look, he turned a more serious, yet happy, one to the screen.

"Captain," he said, "your crew has not only accomplished your mission, but saved our system. Let us escort you to the Clicha homeworld where you can make repairs. And, of course, you are all invited to the wedding!"

***

Captain's Log, Intergalactic Date, 676776.76

The Impulsive has been repaired, courtesy of the Clichan and Kandor empires. The Union has been informed of the battle and has dispatched a janitorial ship to clean up the debris before it becomes a hazard to travel or attracts other Cyber ships.

As for our mission, there was a brief scare when the bride and groom had a fight the night before and called off the wedding, but the groom's wise granny intervened with some timely wisdom, and the two made up just in time for the ceremony. It was beautiful. They wrote their own vows. Petru cried. Best of all, Lieutenant LaFuentes did not have to dash in at the last minute and throw himself at anyone's mercy, nor did Lieutenant Loreli need to inject herself with imposazine, although Doctor Pasteur did treat the wedding party to .1cc's each. Their skin never looked better.

The entire crew was invited to the reception, and since it lasts three days, everyone will have a chance to let off a little steam and enjoy our victory. With the Einstein batteries charged and Deary providing the specs, we were able to treat everyone to an earth delicacy – stout.

The grand ballroom held fifteen different buffet tables, three dance floors with different bands, and ten kegs from the Impulsive. Crew and natives mingled like old friends at the buffet tables and danced like they'd just met and wanted to get to know each other better. Deary held court at one large table where he'd set up a holographic display of the wikadas blade and was lecturing the attending engineers and military commanders on its many unique purposes. Dour, meanwhile, held another audience in thrall with the metaphysics of teleportation. He wore his black robes for the occasion; a few of the bridesmaids watched him intently, their elbows on the table and chins on their fists, occasionally sighing dreamily. Wrapped up in his discussion of the Science and Dark Art of Transmitting Matter, he didn't notice.

Meanwhile, Prince Petru's black-sheep uncle, Sli, had cornered the captain and first officer to talk about the Impulsive and brag about his own military exploits. In between praising the beer, of course.

"Thish stuff is amazing!" he declared as he sloshed a mug of beer in Captain Tiberius' direction. He was on his fifth pint and had already declared half the male crew his best friends and made passes at more than half of the female crew.

"I want to have more," he said. "Long term, I mean. Shet up manufacturing, you know what I mean?"

"You'd have to take that up with Commander Deary," Smythe said, leaning away from Sli's breath. "It's his family's recipe. They have intergalactic patents, I believe."

"Patent-schmatent. I'm sure we can come up with an equitable agreement." Sli tilted his head back and drained his drink. Then, his eyes rolled into the back of his head, and he fell backward. Some of the nearby guests squealed or yelped with alarm. A few of the Impulsive crew, who had had a couple of pints themselves, fell into giggles. Four servants set their trays aside and hurried to grab the unconscious man and carry him to his chambers.

Jeb tapped his comm badge, which only by coincidence looks like a beer glass with a six-pointed star. "Captain to the doctor."

"I see him," the doctor replied cheerily. "Nothing .7cc's imposazine can't help – five, if they want him to keep the hangover."

As they watched the doctor follow the group out, Councilman Edor approached with Doall in tow. The ops officer was blushing even though she'd only had half a glass of Kandor champagne.

Edor said, "Captain, I cannot praise the brilliance of your crewman enough."

"But, really, you already have," Doall replied. With her eyes, she begged for the captain to make him stop.

"No, I agree. You did a hell of a job in the battle," Jeb started, but Edor waved his hands dismissively.

"Battle, schmattle. I'm talking about how she planned to engineer the reunion of the prince and princess. It was sheer genius."

"We never enacted the plan," she protested yet again.

"True, Ellie. Events took their own turn, but what you said in that briefing room. It was inspired! Inspired, I say. You have an understanding of our people that is unparalleled by any in your species. Captain, I'm requesting that you relieve Ensign Doall of her commitments to your ship and let her come to Clicha as your Union ambassador."

"And Captain," Ellie said, "I've been trying to convince him that I'm not senior enough. Besides, I like my job."

"Nonsense! Captain, tell her..."

From a short distance away, LaFuentes and Loreli sipped at their mugs and watched the goings on with amusement.

"Enigo," Loreli said, "the Prince is happily married. I'm no longer under threat of his attentions. You should go have fun."

"There're plenty of security threats aside from Petru. Gotta stay vigilant. Besides, who says I'm not having fun?" he asked, but when she raised one perfectly pruned eyebrow, he relented. "Okay, fine. I'd rather be dancing. So, let's go."

"Enigo, my job as xenologist is to observe the rituals of other species, and as ship's sexy…"

"…it's to be competent, aloof, and admired. I know. But you will be both better able to closely observe and to be admired on the dance floor. You've got to be a competent dancer. Come on. I know how to hurricane."

Her face softened with surprise. "You know the dances of my people?"

"*Claro.* You think all we did on the Hood was fight? Come on, what do you say?"

"Well… if it would contribute to morale…"

"Certainly improves mine." He held out his arm fist up so FEAR showed on his knuckles. She covered it with her hand, and they moved to the dance floor.

The two took the center of the dancers, raised their arms and began to sway in time to the music. Soon, others joined in. From where she rocked in Petru's arms, Katrin pointed and giggled at the group. Petru whispered something in her ear, and the two rose to leave.

Now imagine the camera panning back from the happy scene: dancers, diners, and of course, the bride and groom giggling their way up the stairs. The mansion grows smaller as we rise, swallowed up by the city, where thousands of lanterns are being released into the sky in celebration. Next, the fireworks – watch out! – and then we are in space, where the Impulsive is stationed in orbit, always falling but never descending, hull new and gleaming, ready for its next great adventure.

Polarity Panic

Captain's Personal Log, Intergalactic Date 676786.68

We're back on patrol again after a brief stop at the Union's station at Argo for some repairs, and to rub it in the face of the Union fleet that we defeated a Cyber hive while they were on a wild goose chase. It was all the funnier that some of the captains didn't have a cultural reference for geese, wild or otherwise. That joke just never gets old. Since everyone wants the secret to our wikadas shields, they had to take it in good humor, so for once, we had minimal incarcerations due to bar fights... with the exception of our chief of security. Lieutenant LaFuentes met someone from a rival gang on the Hood, and well. I can't blame him; he was still on edge after nearly having to throw a fight with the Clichan prince.

Fortunately, Ensign Doall was able to convince the magistrate that a knife fight is considered a cultural greeting on the Hood and punishing the participants was inherently racist, so both he and Lieutenant Deisel had their charges dropped from "attempted murder" to "littering" and were fined the cost of cleaning up the blood they spilled in the passageway.

On a side note, between this and her work with the Clichans, Doall has been contacted by the Diplomatic Corps. They think she has a promising career as a diplomat. That'd be a shame. She's too good an ops officer. Damn glad I followed cliché and put her on the bridge crew ahead of more senior and experienced officers.

"Captain?" Ensign Ellie Doall's voice over comms interrupted his musings. "We're picking up subspace anomalies."

"Cybers?" Captain Jebediah Tiberius asked, dropping his feet from the desk. He had hoped they'd be done with Cybers for a few episodes.

She laughed. "As if! We'd be on red alert already. No, sir. But there is a ship in the center of it. They could be in trouble. Commander Smythe has hailed them, but it's a new species. He requests the honor of your presence for when the translator has figured out what they're saying. Poll has three-to-one odds for it being a distress signal."

"Put me down for failed weapons experiment. I'm on my way."

* * *

"Captain on the bridge," Doall said just as the lazivator doors opened. One day, Jeb would figure out how she did that with her back to the doors.

"Report," he said as he entered and made his way to the comfy seat.

His first officer took that time to finish the last of his tea, then answered. "Definitely a distress signal.

Translators are finishing up now. Very idiom-rich language. It appears to be a highly religious species."

He lifted a finger in command and Doall played the transmission. "Oh, Keptar! Save us! Whatever we did, we take it back! By your buttock, bring us aid!"

The transmission continued along those lines, with some gibbering.

"Buttock?"

"The computer insists that's accurate."

"Be sure to keep as many of the original idioms as possible. Loreli will want to study them when she gets back from her conference. Can we transmit?"

"They should be able to understand us now," Doall said.

"This is Captain Jebediah Tiberius of the HuFleet HMB Impulsive. We've heard your distress call. Can we help?"

There was a moment of subspace crackle just to remind the audience that communications weren't always easy or immediate, and then a voice gargled, "Our prayers are answered! Praise Keptar! Our ship has suffered a warp core breach. We must evacuate. Can you get to us in time?"

In the background, a computerized voice announced twelve minutes to get their affairs in order before meeting the Great Crack in the Sky. Doall tagged that phrase for their xenologist.

Space Traipse: Hold My Beer, Season 1

"Well?" The captain asked his helmsman.

Lieutenant Tonio Cruz's hands flew over his console with the grace with which he flew the ship. "Lots of subspace wake, but *va bene*. Plotting the course now."

"I'm sure it will be no problem. How about if we fix your ship instead?"

"Do you know Graptarian technology?"

Tiberius looked at his engineering officer. Lieutenant Morange was a Heptite, skilled, experienced and on the Impulsive for career broadening. He would make a good chief engineer someday soon, but the way he raised all three of his eyebrows clearly said, *Are you out of your mind? We just met this species.*

Jeb liked that his crew felt comfortable being so honest. Still, Morange had a thing or two to learn. He told the Graptarian captain, "We'll improvise."

"Improvise? In ten minutes?"

Maybe the Graptarians were distantly related to the Heptites. "It's what we do."

The translator did a good job of imitating the strain in the alien captain's voice. "I swear by Keptar's left buttock that my own crew has done everything possible. Please – just help us escape. Do not add your deaths to our souls' burdens."

"I'm sure we can multitask. Prepare to receive visitors. Impulsive out. Number One, care for an outing?"

"I could use a stretch. The usual away team?"

"Oh, let's send them the best, and Lieutenant Morange, too. I'm sure Deary can use the assist. And it'll be good career broadening. I'll meet you in Teleporter Room One."

In the bullpen that held the crew of second-string bridge officers, high fives were exchanged, and the secondary engineer took the place of her discomfited Heptite superior. Her heart swelled with pride and ambition. One day, she vowed, she would wear that same deer-in-the-headlights look as her commander chose her for a dangerous and most likely fatal away mission.

As he left the bridge for the head, Tiberius smiled to himself. The Graptarians seem like such a noble species. He had no doubt they'd tried everything possible to save their ship.

Just not everything *humanly* possible.

* * *

The away team boarded the teleporter pads, excited for First Contact and ready for the challenge of repairing the damaged ship. All except Lieutenant Morange, that is. Like the Logics, Heptites were rational, mathematical creatures, and when he'd run the odds of survival, he's almost elected to duck into an airlock, suit up, and blast himself toward the nearest sun in hopes a friendly,

Space Traipse: Hold My Beer, Season 1 ☙ 81

familiar species would pick him up before his air ran out. The odds of survival were somewhat better.

On the way to the teleporter room, he'd mentioned this to Lieutenant LaFuentes, the security officer, who insisted they were too pretty to die but had relayed his findings to Ensign Doall for the latest ship's pool.

His commander had told him he'd learn a lot about humans while serving on the Impulsive. Somehow, he didn't think this is what he'd meant.

Commander Angus Deary hummed to himself as he bumped the spanner on his thigh in time to the music.

"What song is that?" the captain asked.

"Voltaire, sir," Commander Deary replied. "The man understood man's role in the universe, he did."

From the teleporter console, Chief Dour cleared his throat. "Subspace is highly polarized due to the Graptarian's malfunction. My mistress leads you on a difficult and perilous path. Perhaps it would be easier if you were silent for the preparations?"

A Heptite subordinate would have spent a day in isolation, meditating on his rudeness while suspended over a vat of man-eating larva for such a comment, but the captain merely rolled his eyes at his chief engineer. Before Morange could experiment with a rude comment of his own, they dematerialized.

They rematerialized to the controlled chaos of a ship in its death throes. The crew, who looked human enough except for wrinkled foreheads and an affinity for shiny jumpsuits, were rushing to and fro, some carrying what looked like tools while others had luggage. The translators worked overtime to record commands, pleas, and prayers as a ship's computer informed everyone that they had eight minutes to live.

Jeb Tiberius clapped his hands together. "Good! We're early. Where do you think the captain is?"

Almost is if scripted, a Graptarian in a slightly more decorated jumpsuit approached them. "I told you not to come!"

Captain Tiberius smiled. "Such nobility. Please. I'm Captain Tiberius. Captain…Ke?"

"Yes. Please. My people are evacuating by escape pods and shuttles. Can you?'

"Oh, absolutely! We're already prepped to pick them up, get them lunch and a tour of our ship and bring them back when my engineers here have taken care of your little problem."

"Our little…?" The captain nodded and threw up his hands, which also had five fingers and looked human except the nails were a thick brown. "Perhaps it is your way to die in the service of others. Come."

They started down a corridor. Lights strobed between yellow and green. LaFuentes asked, "So is that normal, or is that your alert?"

"It is our highest alert – a call to fleeing and prayer."

Space Traipse: Hold My Beer, Season 1 🎇 83

"*Fantastico*. See, in human culture, green means 'Go' and yellow means 'Go faster.' Of course, it also means it's safe, so you know, kinda opposite."

The alien captain led them to a door just as it opened to a swarm of Graptarians. They froze at the sight of their captain.

"There's nothing else we can do!" The one holding the door panel open said.

Deary raised his box of spanners. "No worries. We brought fresh ideas."

"Meh, I want your best five engineers to stay. The rest, flee!" the Graptarian captain ordered.

Apparently the best five were in the back of the group. They swallowed hard, their coincidentally humanish Adam's apples bobbing in their necks, and made their way to their consoles.

* * *

Inside the engine room of the Graptarian ship, the alarm lights had steadied to a soothing bright yellow. While the computer still counted down to their inevitable demise, the lack of panicky crewmen – save the five silently weeping at their consoles – had made things more relaxed. Jeb felt this was the right time to introduce his away team.

"Captain Ke, Meh, let me introduce my team. Commander Deary, our chief of engineering and his first assistant, Lieutenant Morange. First Officer Phineas

Smythe, who is here in place of our xenologist. She'll be so sorry to have missed this opportunity. My Chief of Security Lieutenant Enigo Guiermo Ricardo Montoya Guiterrez LaFuentes. Doctor Guy Pasteur."

The doctor gave a small, nondescript nod and pointed his scanner in the direction of the one crewman who had gotten a hold of his emotions, as well as his own buttocks. "Don't mind me. I'll be over there taking readings and basically being irrelevant to the current situation. Holler if Angus shocks himself on the alien equipment."

Ke looked at each member of the Impulsive away team, befuddlement growing on his face. "Is this your senior staff? Who's running the ship?"

"Ensign Doall, thanks for asking. Real up-and-comer. I felt the taste of command might do her good, motivate her to stay in HuFleet. Don't worry. She'll make sure your crew's all picked up and fed, and I told her to warp out of here if we didn't have this fixed in..."

"Warning: Warp core breach in four minutes."

"...three minutes. No doubt she'll dally an extra minute or two. You know how junior officers can prevaricate."

Behind him, Smythe muttered, "Doall, prevaricate?"

"We're so screwed, man," Lieutenant LaFuentes agreed.

The captain ignored them both. Commander Deary had wandered over to the main engineering console, which he recognized because it was where Chief Engineer Meh kept glancing with that pensive look, which coincidentally looked just like the pensive look he often saw on human engineers' faces when facing a similar situation. (In simulation, of course, although there was that one time...but we must never speak of it.)

Meh said, "We've tried everything possible already."

"Sure, just not everything *humanly* possible."

"Why should that matter? Do you know how Graptarian warp drives work?"

"Ach. The physics is all the same. Your engines make the same warble that rises in tone – woo wee-eeeee. And your consoles are similar. Flat, like ours. So this squiggly line is the reaction mix interface."

"Yes..."

"So if we just..."

"Don't touch that!"

"Morange, go crack open that console. The one by the guy who's got his hands on his arse. No – the console next to the glowy one. Didn't you learn anything during your safety course? 'If the panel's burning bright, open the one on the right.'"

"What are you doing?" Meh asked. The quality of his voice said that the answer probably didn't matter as it could only add to the insanity, but morbid curiosity compelled him to ask. Graptarians had very expressive tones, not unlike humans.

Like often happens with humans, the tone was lost on Deary, as he studied the console intently. "Well, I think we should reverse the polarity."

"The what?"

"Polarity. Of the magnetic containment field."

"There is no magnetic containment field!"

"No? Well, let's try it anyway. Morange, are there red wires and white wires?"

"Um...yellow and blue?"

"Close enough. Rip them out and get ready to switch them. I want to make a few adjustments here." His fingers flew over the console at a mad pace. Either he'd become an instant expert in Graptarian systems, or he had no idea what he was doing.

* * *

In the debate of whether Angus Deary was an idiot savant or just an idiot, Meh chose idiot. He reached for the Impulsive's engineer's hands, somehow managing to miss. "Stop it! You can't do that. It doesn't even make sense."

Deary paused long enough to bat his hands away. "It's called improvising. I got this, just hold my beer."

"Hold your...what?"

"It means step back and relax. I got this. Morange, ready?"

"Warning: Warp core breach in three minutes, fifteen seconds. Please hang onto your butts and prepare to approach the Great Crack in the Sky."

The alien captain sighed. "Meh, just leave him. It no longer matters. Captain Tiberius, it grieves me that you would sacrifice your ship and all your crew to save us. Maybe if you beamed here, you could beam us all back now?"

"Sure, we've got some time. Away team to Impulsive teleporter room. Get a lock on all the life forms in this room and be ready to zap us out on my command."

"No."

"No?"

"My mistress does not know you."

"Well, get on it! Captain out. I'm sorry, Ke. That's my teleporter chief's fancy way of saying he can't get a lock. But I'm sure Commander Deary will have this done in a jiff."

Sparks flew from the console, and Morange was tossed back. With a yelp of surprise (and perhaps a bit of joy about being useful in this final scene), the doctor rushed to his side. He ran the scanner over him and said grimly, "He's dead, Jeb. Fortunately, his species can handle death temporarily. I can stabilize his molecular makeup with 65cc's imposazine, but we have to get him to a resuscitation chamber in the next four minutes or he's unrevivably dead for sure."

"Anytime, Mr. Dour," the captain said over the communicator.

Smythe took Morange's place while Lieutenant LaFuentes helped the doctor drag the body of Morange out of the way.

"Warning: Warp core breach in two minutes. Please join me in prayer: O Great Keptar..."

Jeb grinned and shook his head. "I knew y'all were a spiritual peo—whoa! Hey, that's my butt you're grabbing!"

The Graptarian captain said, "It's our way. Keptar, seat of all that comes and goes..."

"Smythe, connect the yellow one. Good. I think I've almost got it. What's this button do?"

The air circulation system suddenly reversed. People's hair pulled toward the ceiling and folks staggered as they fought to keep their hands tightly clamped to their cheeks.

"Ooops. Maybe this..."

The aliens chorused,"...and guide us past the bladder of purification and on to..."

The computer started to announce imminent breach.

Deary shouted, "Got it! Plug in the blue one!"

Smythe did so with only a minimal amount of sparking. It was if his British heritage had affected the very wires, preventing them from any garish displays of pyrotechnics.

The engines ceased making a whine like a distressed TARDIS with the emergency brake on. The lights went from warm yellow to a bright florescent white. The computer said, "Warp core has been stabilized. Keptar has heard your pleas. Praise Keptar, whose mercy is sweet but whose wrath is silent but deadly."

"Praise Keptar!"

Meh unclenched and looked over the console. "I... I don't understand... What have you done?"

"Like I said. I reversed the polarity of the magnetic containment field."

"But we don't have a magnetic containment field."

Deary smirked. "You do now. Do you want me to get rid of it?

"No!" every alien and even the computer shouted.

"Didn't think so."

The communicators chirped. Doall's voice spoke cheerily, "Captain, subspace has stabilized. Is everyone all right?"

"Ensign, I told you to get that ship out of here."

Although he spoke sternly, Captain Tiberius grinned and winked at Ke.

"Oh, I know. I was going to, but the bridge crew refused to go until the one minute mark and by then

Cruz was telling a story, and you know how he talks with his hands."

"Ah, we have to do something about that. At any rate, it's a good thing you stayed. All's well that ends well. Have we got teleporter lock? Good. First, beam the doctor and Morange straight to Sickbay. Don't worry; he's just mostly dead. Then teleport over an engineering team – and make sure they bring some magnets with them. We've got a lot we can teach our new friends and a lot we can learn from them, too."

To Ke, he said, "So, tell me more about this Keptar."

As the small engineering crew started to clean up the mess, Captain Tiberius put a friendly arm around the Graptarian captain's shoulders, and like two friends who'd known each other forever, they walked out of the engine room. The door closed as Ke was saying how Jeb had the right tush for worship – firm, yet squeezable.

Captain's Personal Log, Intergalactic Date 676789.07

After two days of working with and learning from our new alien friends, we are leaving them and continuing on our mission. It's been a wonderful experience. Deary got to teach a new crew a thing or two about warp engine technology. Doall has taken her inability to get Cruz to stop waving his arms and steer the ship as a sign that she's not ready for the Diplomatic Corps. Morange recovered and feeling he's learned everything he needs to know about humanity, has requested to return to the Heptite Corps ASAP. The doctor came to the bridge to share a cameo and a joke, but we were all pretty busy.

For me, however, this mission has been a life changer. Never have I felt so close to the divine. I don't think it was the near brush with death. Not like I haven't been there before! But the spirituality of the Graptarian people, even in the crisis, moved me. In the past two days, I've seen it expressed in their routine activities, too. Never have I been goosed so often or with such love. I think...I think I may have found a religion I can embrace.

The captain ended his log. He looked around his quarters, dimmed for the night. The Graptarian ship hung outside his window. As he watched, the drives cycled in the saucer-like vessel and it disappeared. He raised a beer to it and wished them farewell.

Then he set down his glass, grabbed his behind with both hands and said, "Great Keptar..."

Foot in the Door

Loreli stood in the center of the clearing, her face toward the suns, her skin drinking deeply of the unique rays produced by the simultaneous sunset and sunrise even as her eyes feasted upon the spectacle of colors. The fronds that served as her hair splayed around her, and she held out her arms, fingers spread the better to enjoy the warmth. She'd shed her fabric clothing for the walk, choosing to style her foliage as a short but modest dress, in order to make the most of the unique opportunity for photosynthesis. A small breeze played with the hem of her skirt, and she felt the changes in barometric pressure and humidity that signaled an incoming storm.

Rain. Real rain. She longed to remain there, to drink in the natural water generated by the biosphere of a perfect planet rather than the reconstitution and purification processes of a starship. Alas, the government of Breeze-rustle-chitter would never sanction it. No alien being was allowed to "steal" any of the natural resources of the world. That meant no drinking the water, no eating the food...even the soil would be removed from her shoes before she left.

"It's paradise," she sighed.

Behind her, the Breeze-rustle-chitter ambassador hummed in agreement. "It is, isn't it? You understand, then, why we are so careful about whom we allow on our planet."

"Of course." She relaxed, her fronds returning to their usual, hair-like style. She turned her back on the double suns and took the ambassador's proffered arm. "I'm immensely honored you would both share this honor and allow me to speak on behalf of the Union of Spacefaring Planets."

He patted her hand with the second of his four arms and led her down a garden trail back to the sealed biosphere that housed alien visitors. "Well, when Doctor Chit-chit-hack-cree heard your lecture, '101 Ways to Save a First Contact Gone FUBAR,' he knew you of all creatures would understand our conundrum with the dominant Union species. Our world is paradise, and we wish no alien contamination to upset that balance. Some species, we believe we can trust to adhere to our rules – the Logics, and your kind. But humans! Humans are just so reckless and sloppy and..."

"I prefer to think of them as impulsive."

"That's the name of the ship you serve on, is it not? Why do you work with these creatures?"

"And it suits them. Oh, humans are indeed reckless and sloppy and very often seem to hear only what suits them. Yet they are creative and intuitive in ways no other species can match. If they don't always consider the consequences, it's often because they are so focused on the prize of their success. If it were not for the humans, I would still be slave to a mad naturopath. Then-Lieutenant Tiberius ignored the orders of the Union and stole me."

"Stole?"

"I was property, cultivated and pruned to serve my master's pharmaceutical experiments. Jeb's impulsive act led to the recognition of my species as sentient."

"Your world is part of the Union?"

"We're not a spacefaring species. I am an exception, raised by mammals as I was. But you see my point? The curiosity of the human Jebediah Tiberius and his stubborn insistence that he was serving a greater good by disregarding his superiors led to my freedom and the independence of my world."

The wind picked up suddenly, ripping dried leaves off a tree and pelting the duo with them. A thorny bush uprooted and tumbled into the path.

Loreli squealed and laughed. "Like a sudden storm. If you can deal with the chaos, you will reap the benefits of the rain."

The ambassador did not seem so delighted. "The natural chaos provided by a world in balance, we can handle. It's the chaos of alien elements we fear – and the humans, of all species, are the most alien of elements, and not just environmentally."

"I understand. It is a risk. If not, we wouldn't need–"

"A hundred ways to fix a first contact gone FUBAR?" The ambassador's mouth mandibles clicked in its equivalent of a smile. He released her arm. "Please, let me clear the path. We should hurry. Even in our perfectly balanced world, storms can be dangerous."

He skittered away on all six limbs to the bush, but when he got there he rose in surprise and defense. "What are you doing here? These are private lands."

A voice Loreli did not recognized answered. "Which you contaminate with alien presence! It should not be here breathing our air!"

"Eradicate the contaminants!" another voice yelled.

"Loreli, run!" the ambassador yelled. He reached to his pocket, whether for a communications device or a weapon, she did not know, nor did she find out. Their attacker shot the ambassador in the thorax. He gave a screech and collapsed.

Then a second shot took her full in the chest. She fell to the ground, unconscious.

As if responding to the violence, the wind rose to gale force. One attacker gave her the most cursory of examinations, and finding no pulse, ran after his brothers.

The rain began to pelt the two bodies.

***

Captain's Log, Intergalactic Date   676795.10

We're en route to pick up our xenologist and ship's sexy, Loreli, who was redirected at the request of the Union Diplomatic Corps to attempt to re-open negotiations with the Breeze-rustle-chitter system, known in HuFleet as Keepout. Keepout is home to an insectoid species, whose name is…computer, insert proper pronunciation here for the "Grumpy Old Neighbor" species and heretofore insert it whenever I refer to them as GONs. Thank you.

It's been over a decade since the Union has had any contact with the GONs, whose environmental xenophobia is legend among the galaxy. They believe their planet to be a perfectly balanced paradise and thus are violently opposed to any potential contamination. Even before the species had confirmed the existence of extra-terrestrial life, they were already preparing planetary defenses to protect from it, just in case. First Contact was apparently an exercise in frustration, particularly since our early translation devices mistook their warning buoys for attempts to reach out to other species.

Over the past decade, slight inroads have been made. We've exchanged ideas and information via remote contact, and some of the GONs have ventured offworld, which is how Loreli caught their attention. Her visit has broken new ground for Union-Keepout relations. One day, a human may set foot on that world thanks to her efforts.

"End entry," Captain Jebediah Tiberius told the computer. Then, he shook his head. He was proud of Loreli. She'd come so far since that scared little sprout he'd rescued against orders. And yet, between her and Doall, the Impulsive could end up reassigned to diplomatic duty. He shuddered. Good thing he had officers like LaFuentes to round things out.

"We're explorers, dammit, not diplomats," he muttered as he left the ready room to the bridge.

"Captain on the bridge," Ensign Ellie Doall called out from her Ops console. No one, however, heard her. They were too busy listening to his First Officer, Commander Phineas Smythe, relate his experience when he was a navigations second on the Tally Ho! as it tried to make first contact with Keepout.

"When the first buoy translated to 'Private property of the Breeze-rustle-chitter,' we thought it was just a territorial thing, so we broadcast our intentions and continued on. Same thing when we got to 'Keep Out,' which is where we got the idea for the Union name for the system. We put up shields when we got to 'Trespassers will be shot.'"

"But you kept going?" someone from the bullpen asked.

"First Contact was our mission, Ensign."

"Then what?"

"Then they shot at us."

"Bueno!"

Lieutenant Enigo LaFuentes blushed slightly when everyone turned toward him. "I just meant, it's refreshing to find a species that means what it says."

"The engineering and medical departments of the Tally Ho! would not have agreed that day," Smythe remarked dryly.

Jeb took his seat in the captain's chair. "Well, let's hope there will be less shooting this time. Ensign Doall, are the buoys still active?"

"Yes, sir, but all are projecting, 'No Soliciting.'"

"Well, we're not selling anything, so I'll take that as a good sign. LaFuentes, prep shields just in case the inner signs get terser. Cruz, take us in nice and slow."

The ship jerked to a stop with such force, people were shoved against their consoles or tossed from chairs. Several of the second-string bridge officers in the bullpen sprung up alert, then flopped back into their seats as each primary crewperson stood up, unimpaired, and returned to their stations.

"That wasn't me, Captain!" Cruz protested before Jeb could ask.

"Hey, y'all." The computer spoke shipwide to get everyone's attention. "Sorry about that, but Union has ordered an All Stop. No alert status – just a 'hold yer horses.' Hang on for further instructions from the captain. Thank you."

"Incoming message from Yiwu Wylson, Senior Administrator of the Diplomatic Corps," Doall said.

Tiberius exchanged a glance with his First Officer, who shook his head. He apparently did not feel comfortable when it came to handling anything to do with Keepout. Normally, Smythe took diplomatic calls...but then again, this did affect the entire ship... Tiberius placed his fist on his open palm. Smythe did the same. Smacking their fists three times, they did a quick game of paper-scissors-rock-redshirt-alien. Smythe chose redshirt while Jeb took paper. The captain scowled; redshirt files paperwork. He'd have to take the call.

"On screen, Ensign," Smythe said.

The harried, round-faced diplomat appeared on the screen. Since this is science fiction and we are dealing with aliens, let me be clear – Wylson's head was round. Volleyball round. Like all Pelotanns, his bald, round head was connected to his squat body by a long neck. He had six eyes equidistant from each other on his face, set

Space Traipse: Hold My Beer, Season 1 ❀ 101

inward but able to bug out when appropriate. His three mouths, each capable of independent speech, were little more than slits, yet agile enough to imitate the language patterns of nearly every known species in the galaxy, including the gaseous extractions of the Huagg. They had no noses to disrupt the smoothness of their faces, but breathed through a hole in the top of their head. (Needless to say, hats are considered lethal weapons on Pelota V.)

With eyes able to take in everything around them, and mouths that could carry on conversations with three different species at the same time, the Pelotanns were uniquely suited as negotiators. They filled over 70 percent of the jobs in the Union Diplomatic Corps despite some species demanding greater representation. For a while, Jeb remembered, there had been an effort by the Huagg to get a greater share of jobs. No one wanted this, of course. Even putting aside the fact that they did not have qualified candidates, no one wanted to negotiate with a species that spoke in farts. Even with the universal translator, it was not a comfortable process.

After much back and forth and attempts to clear the air, the Union finally insisted they meet with a Pelotann representative to discuss it. The Huagg left agreeing to stay out of the diplomatic corps completely and were happy about it.

This diplomat, however, looked anything but happy. One face frowned at the screen while a second was ensconced in a privacy box on some other business. The third seemed to be working off stress; its tentacles were weaving some kind of intricate doily.

The captain matched his frown to the one on Wylson's face. "You can't have them."

"Impulsive, you are ordered to...what?"

"Doall and Loreli. They're my best officers and you can't have them."

"Aw, thank you, sir," Doall muttered.

"Who said anything about your officers?"

"You instituted a computer-override All Stop on my ship, didn't you? Why else would you hold my ship hostage unless you wanted my people for your diplomatic corps?"

"Very droll, Captain, but I've read your records. No, Captain, I am not interested in your people. I am trying to forestall an interplanetary incident."

"We have permission — and orders — to approach Keepout. They've even changed the warnings — downright welcoming compared to the past. Lieutenant Loreli — whom you can't have — has been working to open visitation rights, something even your kind hasn't been able to accomplish."

"Well, I regret to inform you that her mission has backfired in a horrific way. Terrorists have attacked her."

"What?" LaFuentes shouted from his place at Security.

Jeb held up a hand to quiet him. "Is she all right?"

"The Breeze-rustle-chitter ambassador is dead."

"What about Loreli?"

"She is alive, despite being hit with what for mammals is a lethal dose of radiation and being left for dead in the annual rise-set storms. Unfortunately, the nature of her survival has become the cause of what could be the worst interplanetary crisis between the Union and Keepout since the Tally Ho!"

Everyone within sight of the viewscreen did their best to look ignorant. No one looked at Smythe, who kept a poker face worthy of his ancestry. From behind, however, LaFuentes cut in.

"So what are you saying? Is she in danger?"

One of Wylson's eyes bugged out just enough to look in LaFuentes's direction. "Lieutenant Loreli has broken the greatest taboo of their planet and in a way that's amazingly intricate."

"Is she in danger?"

Wylson waved a tentacle at the screen. "This is why your ship is at All Stop, Captain. I will not have you barging in until we've assessed the situation and determined the dangers, not only to your officer, but to the Union."

"LaFuentes, stand down," Jeb said. "You'll have to forgive my officer. 'The Ship Is Family,' is the motto of our Security Section. He takes the welfare of everyone on this crew seriously."

"Commendable, of course. Let me reassure him and all of you that we are doing everything in our considerable power to rectify this situation. In the meantime, I think…yes… we've arranged for you to talk to your officer and have visual communication. In this case, an image is indeed worth a thousand words."

***

The briefing room of the Impulsive held a barbell-shaped table, each end equipped with a 3D holographic display in the center of the "bell." The shape was really an attempt to make the Modern Arts class at the Academy relevant, but it did serve its purposes. Sometimes, two teams could work on a problem, one at each end of the table, then meet in the long middle to discuss their ideas.

This, however, was not one of those times.

The senior staff sat on one side of the table. Of course, it should be noted that "senior" is used loosely, since several other officers on the ship outranked Ensign Doall and Lieutenant LaFuentes, including three of the Engineering staff, and none of the people in attendance were over the age of 45. Smythe, the eldest, was older than Jeb by five years...unless they were picking up women, in which case, Jeb claimed to be somewhere between 27 and 34, depending on what he thought sounded hotter. Since he'd found Keptar, he'd come to realize that age was not as important as keeping one's gluteus maximus strong and supple...but then again, that had always been a priority for him, anyway.

Right now, however, he hoped to Keptar that he could dig his xenologist out of the fix she was in, literally as well as figuratively.

Loreli looked at them all through the camera that a very irate GON had placed for her so she could communicate. To everyone's relief, she was alive, though not well. Her normally green skin was tinged yellow, and her fronds drooped. Her arms hung limply, though her fingers were splayed to take in the light of the single sun.

Her legs were embedded in the ground, where her feet had transformed into roots that stretched through the planet's rich soil.

The GONs had surrounded her in a force field bubble that allowed only the passage of air. The field seemed to pass through the ground as well.

"I'm so embarrassed about this, Captain," Loreli said. Around her, scientists of the world were taking measurements and soil samples and scowling. In the background, they could hear angry chants. The words were too faint to be intelligible, but Jeb didn't like the tone. By the way LaFuentes clenched his fists, he didn't either.

"What happened?" Doall asked. Despite her years of friendship with the Botanical, she had never seen Loreli revert to her plantlike state.

One of the scientists within earshot of Loreli's screen dropped the soil sample he was taking, an obviously deliberate act, since two of his four legs were empty at the time. He marched to the camera, somehow causing his delicate legs to make angry, distinct stomps in the moist soil, and stuck his face in front of the lens. His words sounded like chitters and hisses.

The universal translator said, "What happened? You know damn well what happened, you fleshy (species-specific expletive here, having to do with the state of your egg before it hatched). We trusted you, and you sent a vegetable to invade our planet."

"Your people attacked me," Loreli responded. "They ambushed me, killed one of your own, and left me for dead. When I woke up, I found myself this way. I didn't intend it. It was an autonomic response of my body to keep me alive. It is because your people did not trust us that we are in this predicament."

Two other GONs pulled the angry scientist away. The translator said they were simultaneously scolding and commiserating with their comrade, though it declined to give a direct translation of what was said.

Every ship in the Union had a filter on the Universal Translator that removed the most potentially volatile conversations when they – in the translator's humble decision matrix – did not pertain to the immediate problem. In some cases, it could replace the more hateful words with less inflammatory equivalents; in other cases, it simply omitted the parts that might set blood boiling and phasers firing. It also condensed longwinded communications, particularly when dealing with impatient species. It was one of the best-kept secrets in Engineering and Diplomacy circles; however one of Chief Engineer Deary's protégés in the AI section had nonetheless heard about it while drinking one of the programmers under the table. He'd come back to the ship, staggering and hung over, but refused the doctor's offer of imposazine until he'd reprogrammed the translator. He couldn't tell it to directly translate everything, but he could introduce a new subroutine to give a loose summary.

"Really," the translator said to the staff, "they're just upset."

Jeb gave his Ops Officer a stern look, but she was already typing away at her pad, shock set aside and anticipating his commands as usual. Once she stopped anticipating what he needed and started thinking for herself, HuFleet would have one hell of a Captain. Until then, he had a few years to reap the benefits of her skill.

"Hell of a way to get your foot in the door, Lieutenant. How extensively have you rooted?" Jeb asked Loreli.

"I'm not sure. I'm trying to stop myself, Captain. I have been ever since I regained consciousness. The force field has actually helped; whenever I touch it, I get zapped." She turned her face slightly toward where LaFuentes sat, fists clenched. "Don't worry; it's just a tickle, really. I don't think anyone wants to hurt me. That would just make things worse."

"The GONs," Jeb trusted the translator to substitute the real name of the inhabitants, "are refusing to let us go to the planet to help you. DipCorps is trying to negotiate something, but in the meantime, I need you to do more than stop yourself. You need to pull those capillaries back in."

"I'll try, Captain. I'm just...so tired."

His voice gentled. "You've been tired before. Refuse this world the benefit of your growth like you did Anora."

She nodded. Out of view of the camera, Doall did the same.

"You've got this, Sprout," Jeb said, reverting to the nickname he'd given her after her rescue. "We'll contact you when we have updates. In the meantime, soak in the sun. Impulsive out."

The screen went dark.

"She did not look good." LaFuentes had an edge to his voice.

Jeb ignored him. "Doall, did you get the readings?"

Her grimace said she had not done as well as she'd hoped, but she put the holographic image of Loreli up for everyone to see. The above-ground section looked clear, though the edges were not as sharp as they should have been. Below ground, there were some large tubular roots with smaller but thick roots growing from them. They were fuzzy, however, and a few light lines indicated more roots too thin to record properly.

"This was the best the sensors can do through the soil. Definitely not good enough for the teleporters."

Jeb nodded. Even if they could teleport just Loreli and not the surrounding soil, she was already in shock. He wasn't sure how well her body could handle the stress of transplanting. He looked at his First Officer. Smythe had been part of the team that made First Contact with Keepout, and he knew he'd kept up on the planet's relations with the Union since.

"They've sealed her from the elements to limit the contagion. The fact that they've let her live seems to imply they aren't sure if killing her won't cause more harm to the environment. In a sense, her natural response to injury has preserved her life."

"And when they decide?" LaFuentes asked. "All those scientists didn't seem to care much about whether she lives or dies so long as they don't contaminate their precious planet. And what about water?"

"They won't water her, even if we sent some ourselves. They'd fear that would encourage her growth."

Jeb held up a hand. "She's safe for the moment. Smythe and I will work with Wylson on a diplomatic decision. In the meantime, I want the rest of you working on a Plan B, C and D. Deary, I want a way to override this All Stop. Cruz, LaFuentes, we need a way to get past their defenses. Doall, work with Chief Dour to find a way to get her back on this ship. If we can do it while respecting the sanctity of their environment, all the better. Get to it, people."

***

Captain's Personal Log, Intergalactic Date 676797.09

You know, I liked the Diplomatic Corp better when they were trying to take my people away for themselves.

We've been negotiating for two days, practically nonstop. The Pelotanns are able to go without sleep for days when necessary, and apparently, the GONs have been perfectly happy to talk with Wylson – who had been given ambassadorial status for this mission – nonstop for as long as he can keep conscious. They've directed him to one bureaucrat after another, on whatever part of the world was on business hours at the time, and Wylson has patiently dealt with each.

Smythe and I, however, are starting to lose ours. We are taking it in shifts to try to work out a solution with the GONs and Wylson, but they will not grant a single concession. They refuse Loreli their water because they will not give resources to an outsider. They won't let us beam in water because they fear contamination. Either case, they say, is out of the question anyway, because they don't want to encourage further growth. They won't let us uproot her, even if we promise to return their soil. They won't let anyone teleport to the planet to examine her and treat the injuries from the attack. They refuse to treat her themselves. On top of that... well, you get the picture.

Loreli, meanwhile, puts on a brave front, but it's obvious she's fading. We may not have time for a diplomatic solution. As my people look for alternatives, I am faced with the worst duty a HuFleet Captain can have – sitting on my hands and waiting.

Jeb ignored the clutch in his stomach as he smiled reassuringly at Loreli. She drooped, her trunk crumpling in on itself. The edges of her extremities were tinged yellow. Her hands, which had been stretched with fingers splayed to take in the sun, hung limp at her side. Her eyes were open to look at the screen, but he felt certain that they would close as soon as they finished talking. He'd make it short, but he wouldn't be doing his job if he didn't call in, just to let her know she wasn't alone. She needed that hope.

He did, too.

"Hey, Sprout, how's it going?"

She smiled thinly but with affection. "You know, you haven't called me 'Sprout' so much since I graduated from the Academy. And I seem to recall when you took me on as xenologist and ship's sexy, you said you'd never call me that again. Something about it 'not fitting the image of a mature, desirable, unattainable woman."

He shrugged. "Well, this whole damsel-in-distress routine has brought out the paternal in me, is all. But I do need a status report, Lieutenant."

She nodded and tried to straighten up. "I've managed to retract most of my ancillary capillaries. I'm working on the greater roots now. It's...incredibly difficult. I'm so thirsty. If I could just have a drink..."

The longing in those words, coming through bark-chapped lips, tore his heart. "I know. But they won't budge. Just keep at it. The more you accomplish, the more we can argue your good faith. I see your trunk is starting to divide. That's good."

He was lying, and they both knew it. True, her trunk had split, and under normal circumstances, that would be the beginning of returning to legs, but the crack was uneven, a tear rather than the carefully considered division of limb generation. Still, even though no scientists wandered around her taking soil samples this late in the evening, he figured his transmissions were being monitored. They may not understand the heroic efforts she was making to fight the survival instincts of her body to root, take in the nutrients of the soil, and survive. He needed them to know. Being a captain was knowing when to lie and how to make it look convincing.

Not to mention, lie though it was, the thought calmed the lump in his throat.

"I'm doing my best, Captain. Enigo called me. He's quite…impassioned…about my situation. Much blustering and vows to rescue me. I don't want him seeing me like this. I… It's not professional."

Yet something in her posture said she'd needed that blustering. Boosting morale went both ways.

"Don't underestimate the power of a damsel in distress. Some males find that very appealing. You know he'd never turn down a chance for thrilling heroics. I'll talk to him about toning down the bluster."

"He's quite distressed himself," she said. Her tone implied enough to do something stupid and against orders.

"We all are, Sprout."

She nodded. She got the message. The Impulsive wasn't below breaking a few regs themselves to save one of their own. Hadn't Jeb done that for a potted plant that turned out to be sentient itself?

Suddenly, there was a loud pattering, and the shield became a dripping gray ball around her.

"It's raining again," she whispered. Her eyes looked past the screen. She trembled.

"Lieutenant?"

She forced herself to look at him.

"We'll figure this out. They aren't going to let you die there. If you decompose, you'd ruin their soil, right?" He hated mentioning the possibility, but did so for whatever enviro-isolationist insectoid lackey was listening.

"It'd be a relief," she admitted.

"We have other relief waiting on the Impulsive. The doctor is mixing up a nice nitrate-laden sludge, and the whole botany department is drawing lots on who gets to prune you."

She giggled. "I'd like crewman Lin to do my hands. She does the best manicures."

"Noted. We'll get you out of this. We're family," he started the Impulsive's motto given to them by Lieutenant LaFuentes.

"And family takes care of its own," she concluded.

***

Captain Tiberius sat braced against the back of the briefing room chair in order to avoid the temptation of resting his head on his fist. He'd just finished eight hours of negotiations with the Keepout's Minister of Environmental Purity, and he was certain they had made up the position special for this crisis. It didn't help; his legs were as tied as everyone else's. The rules were plain: No outsiders could contaminate their beautiful world. This incident was exactly their worst fears come true. Never mind their own people instigated it.

I swear, those terrorists are getting exactly what they want, Jeb thought.

At least he had acquiesced to letting them scan Loreli through the comm link. Doctor Pasteur had just finished his report on Loreli's health. "Of course, this is just the roughest of examinations," he concluded. "If only we could get her some nitrates and a couple ccs of imposazine…"

"A couple?" If the doctor was guessing at dosages, it was worse than he thought, and Jeb knew Loreli better than anyone. He's seen her at the height of health and at the withering brush of death. He knew she was in a bad way.

"I can't tell from the scans, but she has internal injuries. She's leaking chlorophyll."

"We're on the clock," LaFuentes said. "Why can't we blast that shield, uproot her, return the soil and let that Wylson work it out after we've warped the hell away?"

Jeb rubbed his eyes. He'd wondered the same thing himself, until Smythe told him about the negotiation session he and Wylson had had with a GON historian. The historian had explained in what the universal translator insisted were very flowery and patriotic terms about how a Kitack trader had made off with a three-foot square of sod. The GON armada had mobilized, destroyed the trader and his allies. All of them.

There had been hand-to-hand combat within one ship, the GON historian had said. Not only had they killed the Kitacks, but the injured GON were euthanized and dissolved so that the alien contamination could be removed and expelled. The remains were returned to the soil.

"Apparently, the area that was 'fertilized,' if you will, by the dead has become quite a lovely commons," Smythe concluded.

Space Traipse: Hold My Beer, Season 1 ⚔ 117

Jeb liked parks, but that was not how he wanted to have one made. "Dour, give me a better alternative," the captain said.

The teleporter chief pulled up the schematic of Loreli they had taken the first day. He overlaid it with a blue outline that covered her aboveground body and only the thickest roots belowground.

He said, "I have delved deeply into the arcane mathematics. Long have I toiled in the internal workings of The Machine. This is the best my mistress sees fit to grant me. If it be enough to save our ship's sexy, say the word."

"What about with the shield down?" LaFuentes asked.

"The problem is the soil. I can no more remove that which sticks to the epidermis than I can separate the sweat off your redshirts after they've been running away from some threat or the other – and trust me, I have tried. Perhaps if I beamed all but a few layers of skin..."

The doctor shook his head. "She's not mammalian. If we strip her roots while she's in such a fragile state, she'll go into shock, and I can't guarantee I'll be able to revive her."

"That's not good enough, doctor."

"Damn straight, it's not!" LaFuentes rose from the table. "We've been at this for three days, Captain.

Enough diplomacy! Let me get a team and go get our sexy back!"

"Enigo," Doall began.

"Don't 'Enigo' me, *chica*! How many stupid scenarios have you run, and you don't have any better plan, either? Where's your miracle worker rep now? Maybe you need to go read another book?"

"LaFuentes, that's enough." Some men roar. Some spoke with quiet anger. When Captain Jebediah Tiberius scolded, it was with a hard drawl that most beings instinctively associated with the cocking of a gun, even when they didn't know what a gun was. It made weak men cower and strong men flinch.

Enigo shut up fast, but he glowered.

"Lieutenant, I think you've been at this too long. I want you to take a break and cool your head. Go spend an hour in the gym."

"What? Captain!"

"Not the firing simulation, either. The gym. Dismissed."

LaFuentes opened his mouth to protest, but Jeb said, "Git," and his Security Chief got.

Good thing, too, because almost immediately after the door closed, Wylson's round head appeared in the center of the table. "Captain! I've been in private negotiations with the head botanist, and they have

Space Traipse: Hold My Beer, Season 1   119

agreed to a compromise. This afternoon, they will return your Loreli to you."

"That's excellent!" Jeb said.

"Just as soon as they chop her down."

***

Grumbling in the mix of English, Spanish and Zepharian that was the language of the Union Genship, The Hood, Enigo LaFuentes stomped his way to the gym, dressed in loose shorts and a tight muscle shirt. He inserted himself into the weights machine. The contraption proudly declared itself a "Bowflex," but he didn't see any bows at all. Rather, a complex series of force fields allowed you to push and pull against whatever weight resistance you set and in all manner of directions. He submitted to a retinal scan and scrolled until he found his Fury Workout. The machine activated and he felt the fields envelop his body. He was lifted from the deck.

"Okay, *benndero*, show us what you got!" The words "Right Hook, 40 pounds, 3 sets of 15" shone before his eyes and his hands and arms grew heavy. In his ears, wild chords started playing while angry men shouted Zephspanglish about guns and lust and long walks among the daffodils in the greenhouse section.

Enigo bobbled his head until he got the rhythm of the song, then he swung.

Soon, as the captain had no doubt anticipated, he was lost in the movements, the repetitions, and the music. His anger moved from an encompassing rage to a low burn that fueled his adrenalin. But even floating leg lifts against simulated three Gs couldn't wipe the image of Loreli's pale face from his mind. She'd put on a brave smile, yet was too tired to make it her signature "You've amused me; you may have a chance if you are very brave and very strong" smirk. Her skin had looked so dry, he thought it would flake off and flutter to the ground like methane snow if he touched her. And he so badly wanted to touch her.

He shook his head, not a great thing to do while trying to bring your knees to your chin in three times your normal gravity.

"Ay!" the computer scolded. "You want to concentrate here? You do these wrong and you throw out your back, *comprende*? How you gonna protect your family on your back like an *invlad*?"

He blinked fast, then sought something else to focus on. Day shift had begun just an hour ago, so many of the mid-shift crew were in the middle of workouts. He saw folks on the treadmills, still a tried and true, their VR glasses and adaptive tread simulating environments and motivations from a relaxing run on the beach to being chased by the dreaded and possibly mythical Gridnak. A couple of his redshirts were practicing falls with simulated injuries – parts of their bodies made useless by the same force fields that held him in place. One noticed him looking and lost her focus, not a good thing when running the "stepped on exploding moss" simulation. She fell hard, and her buddy laughed, until he, too, lost his footing and ran instead of jumped off a cliff. Even simulated belly flops were a bitch.

In another corner, Minion First Class Gel O'Tin was running an obstacle course set up specifically for his species. Rather than going over, under and through obstacles, Gel had to go around them in the most literal way possible, by absorbing them into his body, then expelling them. He must be frustrated, too, because he set up an especially difficult course. After some bulky objects to warm up, he moved to more complex objects containing multiple angles and textures until the piece de resistance (literally): Pipes, the Engineering Department's pet katt.

Early in space colonization, humankind learned that no matter how carefully they packed, critters sometimes still got on ships. The solution was to introduce a predator. Sure, they could make robots, but humans still loved their fuzzy animals, so ambitious geneticists and breeders worked together to make the perfect shipboard companion, the katt. Lean and agile enough to navigate the tightest spaces, intelligent yet docile, and with a ravenous appetite and a resistance to a multitude of venoms, it made the perfect predator for capturing bugs and small animals that stowed away on supply crates or shuttles. It had long claws for defense, prehensile toes and tail for climbing surfaces, and an almost pathological need to "go" only in the kattbox.

They also had a great need for cuddles. Pipes was always up for sitting on a crewman's lap, and his silky fur and gentle purr soothed many a distressed spirit. Enigo had even heard that some ships had multiple creatures just for comfort. Of course, he knew Gel's plans for the unsuspecting katt had nothing to do with petting and muttering sweet nothings.

Gel had coaxed Pipes to stay still with a bowl of kibble. The katt stood with his back to the security officer, content and nibbling as Gel adeptly absorbed and expelled a rock, then a wire basket, then a bag of rocks...

When Gel wrapped a gooey pseudopod on the katt's tail, Pipe's head jerked away from his bowl. His low growl became a howl of rage as the Globbal raced up his haunches and over his stomach. Too late, Pipes tried to scramble free, claws flexing and scrambling for purchase. His flailing upset the food bowl, spilling kibble, which were pulled into Gel's bulbous form. Gel's slurp cut off Pipes' screech.

Frozen in shock and indignity, his eyes wide and his limbs still splayed for flight, the helpless katt seemed to travel across Gel's body as he pushed him through his system. Around him people were at once laughing and scolding him.

As Gel's commanding officer, Enigo forced himself not to guffaw. Besides, he knew the kind of effort and skill it took to absorb and expel a living creature alive. Not to mention all of Pipes' fur and those razor-thin claws. On top of that, he had to extract the kibble from its claws, some of which had been ground to a fine dust...

"Computer, halt program!"

"Oh?" the Bowflex taunted, "had enough already, babimann?"

"Shut up, and let me down." As soon as his feet touched the ground, he shoved open the door and ran to his minion. "Gel, spit out that katt and come with me. We need to talk to the captain!"

***

LaFuentes, Gel, and a mollified Pipes emerged from the turbolift onto the bridge.

"We have to talk to the captain!" LaFuentes declared.

"Enigo!" Doall said. "The captain told you to – oh!" She took in his gym attire and sweaty...everything. And he had a jar of dirt. Then her eyes traveled to Gel, who didn't wear gym clothes or clothing of any kind, but was still worth a gander because he was cradling the ship's katt, who had apparently decided to forgive him in return for snuggles. Pipes blinked sleepily and purred.

"Okaaay," she said.

Smythe turned in his seat just enough to make eye contact. From the lack of surprise he showed, one would think the two – three – bursting in was nothing unusual. And to be frank, stranger things had suddenly appeared on the bridge of the Impulsive; it was just they were usually unknown aliens. "The Captain is in negotiations and cannot be disturbed. I take it, however, you have an idea?" He tapped a quick message to the captain on his console: Keep stalling.

They descended to the main floor. The entire bridge crew set their consoles on "distracted user" and turned to watch. This setting directed the computer to alert them if anything on their consoles needed their attention and allowed them to take part in the drama that made bridge duty so desirable while ensuring the ship didn't get invaded or blown up because someone wasn't focused on their jobs.

"Pretend Pipes is Loreli. So the big deal is that they don't want us making off with any of their oh-so-sacred dirt, right?"

"Rather sarcastically put, but essentially correct."

"And we can't transport her without some kind of protection for her roots because she's too fragile, right?

Not to mention her roots are thin and tangled in the dirt."

"I assume you are stating the obvious for the benefit of the bridge crew who have not been part of the planning session."

"Yeah, sure. Oh! Right. I'll get to the point. Watch." He opened the jar, got his hand dirty and then petted Pipes, leaving a brown streak on his sleek tortoise-shell fur.

"Go ahead, Gel."

Gel ran a pseudopod over Pipes' dirty back. He lifted his arm, pulling the fur up with him to show he had enveloped it, soil and all. Then the substance inside his pseudopod began to shift. Little by little, the dirt flowed off of Pipes and out the back of Gel's pseudopod until he held a clean katt and a ball of dirt. He put it back in the jar, and gave LaFuentes a high five. His pseudopod surrounded his boss's hand, and like before, drew off the dirt. This, too, he deposited.

"Computer, how much dirt did we lose?" LaFuentes asked.

"Just like the last three times, there's no discernable difference," the computer obliged.

This time, the security chief and his minion gave each other a real high five. It made a splotchy, wet sound, the sound of victory.

"Impressive," Smythe admitted.

LaFuentes grinned his mad, I-got-this! grin. "Even better, we don't have to uproot Loreli at all. Gel can just infiltrate the soil, surround her roots, and extract the dirt. Then Dolfrick can zap them out together."

"It's no problem, Captain," Gel added. "I can wrap myself around our ship's sexy easy."

There were a few sighs and some jealous mutterings among the bridge crew.

Smythe ignored them. "Gentlemen, you may have saved Loreli's life and earned yourselves some extra leave. Now get cleaned up and prepare for another demonstration in case the captain needs to convince the GONs. And get Pipes some milk. He has been a good kitty."

* * *

Jeb's momma used to tell him, "You'd better corral that temper of yours, boy. Stampedes don't do anything but damage."

Jeb's dad used to say, "Stampedes are what cattle do. We're men, not cattle."

It took him a few years to figure out what his dad meant, but he'd learned there was a time for temper, and a time for damage — or at least the promise of damage. He was at that point now.

When Wylson had called with his "good news," Jeb had dismissed his officers with the order to "Get me an

Space Traipse: Hold My Beer, Season 1 ❈ 127

answer – and prep a stealth shuttle with Wikadas shields in case you don't."

Next, he arranged for Smythe to listen in on his negotiations through a private com link and gave him a "go" phrase. He would stall as long as he could, but if he said the phrase, then Smythe was to launch whatever rescue operation they'd managed to come up with.

Then he'd gone to his ready room and contacted Wylson and the GON who'd come up with the cockamamie idea of chopping down his xenologist. He sat at his desk so his frustration didn't show in physical activity. If he had to stampede, it would be with words...and phasers, if need be.

He'd tried to reason with them. He'd shown them medical records and the Loreli's health readings. He'd even tried to compromise to uprooting and a power wash, though the Botany Department wasn't sure she could survive that. He was getting dangerously close to a stampede.

"Tell you what, Whoosh-chit-chit-kreee. How about if you come to my ship, and I cut off the bottom half of your thorax with an ax?"

Wylson's frontal features fought for neutrality, but his right-side face stifled a snicker. Apparently, it was fed up with the GONs as well. Whoosh-chit-chit-kreee, gasped.

"Are you threatening me?"

"I think," Wylson cut in, while his side face put a tentacle to his mouth and pretended to cough, "that Captain Tiberius is drawing an analogy to the injury such an action would do to his valued officer."

"Though if a threat works..." Jeb added.

The GON waved a leg. "Nonsense! She's a vegetative life form. A plant! Get her into a fertilized bath and she'll be fine."

"Maybe if we'd done so immediately," Jeb agreed. "Maybe if you'd let us heal her injuries. But she is perilously weak, bleeding internally –"

"Plants don't bleed."

"Vegetative life forms do. She is a living, sentient creature. She's not some orchid you can take a cutting from."

The GON did an admirable job of pretending to roll his eyes.

Jeb opened his mouth to give the "go" phrase and to hell with diplomacy, but a message appeared on the bottom of his screen. *Keep stalling*. He grit his teeth and corralled his temper. He needed to give his people more time.

***

Captain's Log, Intergalactic Date 676797.50

Hottdam if my security officer didn't come up with an elegant solution to our conundrum. Never underestimate the inspirational power in a good workout.

We performed our little demonstration for the GON botany team, and after some careful measurements and a virtual sampling of Minion O'Tin's bodily matter, they declared themselves satisfied that our plan will respect their requirements for environmental purity while letting us get Loreli out alive. The Impulsive's own botany team has worked with Doctor Pasteur to create an optimal strengthening fluid for Loreli. Minion O'Tin has absorbed some of this into his own body so that he can share it with Loreli once he has enveloped her root system. He's also absorbed some quantum trackers so that our teleporter chief can lock onto all of Loreli's roots for teleportation.

The DipCorps has released the All Stop on my ship, and the GONs have stood down their planetary defenses.

The GONs have even set up a platform where we can beam down and oversee the process without stepping on their soil. Apparently, they are going to have some dignitaries there to talk about how this is a great step forward in Union/Keepout relations. Wylson will speak remotely on behalf of the Union, which is only fair since I did suggest taking an ax to one of said dignitaries.

So, it's looking like All Systems Go for a nice, easy conclusion. Which is why the ship will be on Yellow Alert, and I've authorized Lieutenant LaFuentes to join us, and we'll all go armed. I don't want to say this has been too easy, but...

In the teleportation room, Lieutenant Enigo LaFuentes handed the captain a weapon. Jeb checked the charge, ignoring his security chief's frown. He'd authorized only energy weapons; they looked cool and ceremonial when paired with the formal dress uniform, and he didn't want to chance spilling any blood. This close to the end of the mission, the last thing they needed was to mess things up by contaminating the soil, after all.

The doors slid open and Minion First Class Gel O'Tin oozed, slug-like, in. His normally green skin was more aquamarine due to the nutrient fluid he'd absorbed. Right behind him, the botany team trundled a vat containing the same fluid mixed with potting soil. It smelled vaguely of manure. Jeb felt a touch of homesickness, but all the same, he was glad his Globbal crewman had not absorbed the smell with the substance.

"I am so bloated!" Gel declared to the room at large. "I haven't felt this full since Union Day."

"That was a party!" LaFuentes agreed. The annual celebration usually included a great deal of alcohol and sometime well into the festivities, someone had suggested "Gel shooters." Gel had obligingly absorbed an entire vat of tequila and offered teaspoonfuls of himself to the daring and adventurous. He's even submitted to being salted so folks could lick him beforehand.

Then LaFuentes laughed. "Who'da thought it would be training for today?"

"Never waste an experience," Jeb agreed. "Are we ready?"

The chief botanist said, "As soon as you zap away, we'll set up the vat to receive Loreli."

Chief Dour said, "Auxiliary teleporters are ready with Plan B."

"Excellent. Let's do this."

Jeb led them to the teleporter platform, but Dour called for them to wait. He fixed LaFuentes with narrowed eyes. "Did you 'go'?"

"What?" LaFuentes sputtered. "You're seriously asking me that now?"

"I respect the GONs' quest to preserve their purity. And your bladder is notorious."

"Whoa, man! Personal!" Yet a couple of the botany team grimaced in agreement with Dolfrick.

"But he has a point," the captain put in. "There are going to be several long-winded speeches."

"Captain, I'm fine."

"I can inspire you, boss," Gel said. "I'm carrying almost two extra gallons of fluids. I am the perfect balance of biological and technological requirements for this mission." The Globbal stretched and lifted the bulk of his girth up in a simulation of sticking out his chest.

"Seriously, Captain. I'm fine."

"Dolfrick, take us down."

The three dissolved as Gel was saying he didn't get paid enough to hold something LaFuentes couldn't hold himself.

The teleporter chief's aim was as true as his devotion to his Mistress of Teleportation, and they arrived solidly on the platform, close enough to Loreli that Gel could stretch himself to her without ever touching the planet itself.

When Jeb saw her, he bit back curses the universal translator would have had to summarize as "expressing deep concern and alarm." In the past few hours, her situation had gone from serious to critical. She had folded over, with what would normally be her knees on the ground and her seat on her heels. She was slumped, her fronds wilted in front of her face. She wasn't even trying to make an affectation of breathing.

She was still surrounded by the force field.

Jeb gave a quick glance at his Security Chief, but LaFuentes was in mission mode, channeling his rage toward finding and cataloguing targets. Gel was subtly inching toward the edge of the platform closest to Loreli. Good.

He turned to the knot of GONs who were politely gathered to one side next to the projection of Wylson. The face toward the GONs expressed calm neutrality, but the one Jeb could see most plainly had his thin mouth compressed in fury. The GONs had decorated themselves with jewels and metallic ribbons on their carapaces and had a teleprompter in between them. They showed no concern at all for the alien dying only feet away from them.

Jeb didn't bother to ask why the shield was still in place. He just demanded they lower it.

One of the GONs, some chief muckety-muck Jeb had not spoken to, stepped forward. "Welcome, crewmen of the Impulsive." He did not sound sincere. "I'm Click-click-kritta-chitter. I'm the elected leader of this province. I'm sorry we didn't speak earlier; I was attending the hatching of my larvae."

"Congratulations. Now release my crewman."

"Thank you. I'm afraid I've assessed the situation myself and I cannot allow it. These are dangerous times for my constituents. You've seen for yourself what the terrorists are capable of, and they have the philosophical backing of the majority, even if we do not agree with their methods. It's a difficult situation."

"Release her!"

"I cannot lower that shield. We will dig her up and transport her to a secure facility where we can carefully extract her under controlled situations."

"She'll be dead by then!"

"But my planet will live contaminant free. You see the greater good here, yes?"

Gel spoke up. "Captain? What if they lower the shields partway, then I can get in and coat her? Their scientists already agreed that's safe."

"No!" another GON shouted. "It's a trick. Look at him. He's not green anymore. He's almost blue! They want to poison our land."

Beside that one, another reached into his pouch and pulled out a weapon. "To arms! Eradicate the contaminants. Keep Breeze-rustle-chitter pure!"

"The Ship is Family!" LaFuentes retorted and shot the gun out of the GON's hand.

Some days, I hate being right. Jeb activated his personal body armor just in time. He felt a slight warmth on his back as the energy beam someone shot him with was deflected.

So much for the easy solution.

Captain Tiberius crouched down to make himself smaller, but, stuck on the platform, he nonetheless made a tempting target. Fortunately, the terrorists seemed to think everyone in the gathering should be shot. Energy streams and projectiles flew at the GON dignitaries from all angles. The insectoid beings were dashing about, seeking cover, clinging to each other and generally panicking and getting in the way of the few security officers they'd brought, just in case. Both GONs and ammunition passed through the holographic image of Wylson, whose neck twisted about while all three heads tried to get a handle on the situation. Finally, he tossed six tentacles in the air, mouthed, "Stay on the platform!" and disappeared.

"Tiberius to Dour. Plan B!"

Lieutenant LaFuentes was in his element. As soon as he'd made his war cry, he had started taking out assailants, some of whom he'd already seen from the trees. (Later, he'd tell the captain he didn't fire on them right away because it seemed undiplomatic.)

Moments after Jeb called for Plan B, several barriers materialized on the platform. Jeb wedged himself between two that gave him the best protection, while LaFuentes used them to dodge behind, jump over and shoot around. He'd tossed a weapon to Gel, who was also doing his share of damage.

Jeb was, too, of course. He couldn't let his crew show him up, but his mind had to be on the real goal of the mission.

"LaFuentes!" he yelled to be heard over the zaps and ploiks and screeching and other sounds of pandemonium. (Use your imagination or recall Starship Troopers fight scenes.) "Make a hole in that shield and cover Gel!"

"On it, Captain! Dour, Gel, get ready for thrilling heroics. For Loreli!" LaFuentes spun to his left and fired at a small box that had been humming away, completely unmolested by the terrorists or the law enforcement. It went up in a shower of sparks. All around them, a wail rose, as if friend and foe (or in Jeb's point of view — foe and more foe) screamed, "No!"

"Gel, move out! Dolfrick, count of twenty-five!"

The Globbal coiled himself like a spring then bounded toward Loreli.

Jeb counted. One, two...

Gel's body stretched then snapped back to its usual blobby shape, wiggling as it arched through the air.

Three, Four...

A stray bullet smacked into Gel at a shallow angle, knocking off a bit of his ectoplasm. It spun away at an oblique angle. Almost in deep slow-motion, Jeb could hear a second scream, "Noooo!"

Five, six...

Jeb grabbed a piece of the platform that had been snapped off in the battle. He flung it toward the broken bit of Gel.

Seven, eight…

The piece of Gel smacked against the board, bounced off it and headed back toward the rest of his body. Gel reached out with a long pseudopod to grab it and suck it back into himself.

LaFuentes yelled, "Dolfrick, ten more seconds!" as he shot the sharpshooter who had tried to injure his minion.

Nine…

Gel smacked against Loreli's chest, startling her conscious.

"Gel!"

"Pardon me, Ma'am. Thrilling heroics. No time to explain. Just, uh, relax."

Loreli squealed and giggled as he spread himself thin over her and oozed down her body.

Twenty three, twenty-four.

The world began to sparkle around them.

Jeb and LaFuentes rematerialized aboard the Impulsive next to the huge stinky vat. The barricades were around them, and Loreli was safely in the slop.

"You're welcome," Dolfrick said.

Weak as she was, Loreli still managed to complain that Gel was tickling her.

Beside her, the slop began to bubble, then a mound of sludge grew. Someone of the botany team gasped, then the sludge sloughed off and Minion First Class Gel

O'Tin, Hero of the Day and the only creature known to get so intimate with their ship's sexy, emerged and glopped out of the vat.

"Sorry for that," he said. "We were in kind of a time crunch. Normally, I like to take things more slowly."

"Ay!" LaFuentes snapped.

Loreli leaned against the vat. Already, her skin was starting to return to a healthier green. "Thank you. You saved me. Against all odds and any logic, you've come through again." She gave each of them a weary, pale, yet completely stunning smile. A couple of the team, including the doctor, blushed. Enigo stuck out his chest.

But Jeb? He was just glad to have his Sprout back aboard.

***

Captain's Personal Log, Intergalactic Date 676798.02

...and as soon as we were aboard, Smythe ordered our hasty exit. We got out of the system before any weapons could mobilize. So far no Keepout forces have pursued. Not the easy solution we'd hoped for but didn't expect, but the successful one we wanted.

Loreli is in a special alcove in Sickbay, still in the vat of nutrients and being misted 'round the clock. She's already looking better. Her trunk is again splitting to legs, and the doctor said she should be ambulatory in a

Space Traipse: Hold My Beer, Season 1   139

few weeks. Engineering set her up with a humidity-resistant console, and she's already hard at deskwork. Which is good. I think she needs the distraction, considering the mission, in her opinion, was such a dismal failure.

I disagree, of course; after all, except for Loreli, who was the victim of a terrorist attack, no member of the Impulsive placed any contamination whatsoever on Keepout. In this whole Human-GON encounter we took the high ground and held it.

I'm going to go talk to her, as soon as I get the debrief from Wylson.

As Jeb looked at the split screen showing all three of Wylson's heads, he marveled that a creature with one brain could hold so many opinions.

Wylson 1 had a call from Keepout and excused himself to take it. The privacy shield was on, but Jeb could see he was agitated. He'd taken control of an extra tentacle just to fling it about in frustration. Meanwhile, the others kept talking with Jeb.

"Are you kidding?" Wylson 2 said to his own other face. "I saw that throw! The Captain just grabbed a piece of, of debris and whirled it at his security officer. It was, as the humans say, Herculean."

"Thank you. And all this time, I'd thought three years of disc golf in high school was only good for getting my sports letter so I could make it to the Academy."

Wylson 3 cut in. "You fired on civilians!"

"We shot at terrorists. They were killing all the dignitaries and scientists, too, you know. Did anyone die, by the way?"

"Apparently, an underling. They didn't mention his name, only that he had a red thorax. But you also destroyed the shield generator."

"Which was the only way we could save our crewman and protect their planet's soil sanctity. We did an analysis and found despite everything, Loreli and Gel combined retained only .0034 grams per cubic meter. That's better than the Logics did at their last visit in '5776. We even ran Gel through the teleporter, removed the rest of the foreign elements and sent them back."

That had been Dour's idea. The security chief was always up for a challenge. A detailed transport at sublight-away through the shields had made his day. Jeb had even allowed him to wear his black robes for a shift to celebrate.

"Didn't they shoot at you?"

Jeb shrugged. "We were too fast for them."

"You went down there armed for a fight."

"We went down there ready to defend ourselves."

"Come on, Wy," Wylson 2 said. "You were facing the other way. The Impulsive officers were amazing – the epitome of everything good about their species."

"Shucks, thank you, Wylson."

"I don't agree!" Wylson 3 said.

"Then, up your third, sir."

The privacy shield around Wylson 1 snapped shut and the head spun around, with protests from the other two. Wylson faced the captain. "This is all a moot point now. The GONs have broken off relations, armed their buoys and recalled all their people."

Jeb raised a brow. He'd expected the reaction from the GONs, but not that Wylson would call them by the human slang. Looked like another head had had their fill of the species.

"Good riddance!" Wylson 2 said.

"Let me talk to them," Wylson 3 argued.

"No. It's done. They need to get themselves in order. The Union has enough drama dealing with humans – no offense."

"None taken. We excel at drama."

"I have let them know that we are willing to reopen channels as soon as they are willing to accept a diplomat of our choice. I think we'll send a Huagg." All the Wylsons smiled a tight, determined smile.

* * *

Despite the shield that was supposed to hold in moisture, Sickbay felt more humid than usual to Jeb. The Doctor was in his office, working on…something. Jeb felt certain he always kept handy a few vials of something colorful to stick in a scanner when he wasn't interested in talking to people. He waved for him to continue his research – real or pretend – and wandered to Loreli's alcove.

She was working on a portable console, her back to the room and earbuds in. Probably Mozart; even among alien plants, human classical music seemed to stimulate growth. Her color was back to its original green, and a seat had been put into her vat. This was a good sign; she had legs rather than a trunk to sustain her.

Jeb rapped on the side of the alcove.

"Captain!" Loreli rose and swished to face him. She was thinner, he saw, her chest not as buxom, but still in a classic athletic form many found appealing. Her uniform was smoother and tighter to match. She was such a professional.

He glanced at her hands. "Lin did a fine job."

She smiled, "And I'm caught up on ship's gossip. Did you really goose Commander Deary?"

"That was on the Graptarian ship. I was newly converted and a little enthusiastic. Enough about me," he said. "How are you?"

Space Traipse: Hold My Beer, Season 1 ❦ 143

She knew he meant emotionally rather than physically. "Lin also told me about Keepout. Of all the missions to go FUBAR, I did not expect it to be by me."

"You didn't do anything wrong, Lieutenant. That was the terrorists. The GONs have some growing up to do before they're ready for the Union."

"I suppose."

"Hey, did I ever tell you about my family?"

"You're ranchers?"

"That was just my direct line. I've got this one umpteenth-great uncle, Grant. He's family legend. Mom said I must have some Uncle Grant in me."

"Oh?" She pulled her chair around. Everyone knew when a senior officer started sharing personal or family stories, there was a moral attached. It paid to listen.

"'It's the wanderlust,' she said. He had it, too, but this was in the time of fossil fuel transportation. He became what they called a door-to-door salesman, traveling around, visiting people and trying to get them to buy his stuff."

"Like I was trying to 'sell' membership to the Union?" Loreli asked.

Jeb nodded. Normally, he'd playfully chide a crewman who interrupted his story to get to the point, but for Loreli, he'd make an exception. "He had a motto that traveled throughout the generations of Tiberiuses:

Sometimes, when you stick your foot in the door, someone'll slam the door on it."

He smacked the side of the alcove, mainly so the author had a definitive transition for him, and pointed at her console. "Don't work too hard. Once you've nursed that sore foot back to health, I expect you back on the road."

"Yes, sir. Thank you, Jebediah."

"Anytime, Sprout."

Day in the Life

In the life of every SF series, there comes a time when it has a "filler episode." You know the type: cute, personality driven, day-in-the-life of some minor character that is more about showing the main characters in a casual plotline that probably does not involve phasers. The episode ends happy and unsurprising, and you may never see the protagonist again. (Unless the audience loves them so much, the actor/actress gets asked to come back and join the life of fame, fortune, and conventions. And if they aren't, they may still find fame and fortune with some other series, but are doomed to go to cons forever pegged as "That girl in the filler episode, um, um… You know, the one where we follow her around the ship doing…something? She was cute, but we never saw her again. Oh, well, it wasn't much of an episode…")

Well, dear readers, we have approached that time here! I promise the character will be cute, as will the vignettes. I also promise there are breadcrumbs important to later episodes, because I hate useless fillers. And if you like the character, let me know in the comments and maybe it'll return.

"It," you say? Read on.

One of the best parts of being in HuFleet is that the only times you have to sweep or dust are while a newb at the Academy or when on a planet trying to fit in with the native population, which is why they still require you to take Primitive Housekeeping 101 at the Academy. The rest of the time, you only need to do such mundane chores if you enjoy it and aren't interested in getting psychiatric help for your delusion.

We open our story on the trail of a Janbot 3000, series 5, as it scurries along the hallways of the Impulsive, following a track only it and the mathematicians who programmed it understand to be the most efficient route. Its tiny brushes whir under its base and on the sidearm it uses to clear the corners, sockets, and baseboard area. The collected dust, microbes, and alien matter are analyzed for potential dangers unnoticed by humans. Any potential threats are reported to Ops and the appropriate science or engineering department. Then the particulates are incinerated, and the resulting energy used to fuel janbot on its way.

Some might say this is impossible, but thanks to the Theory of Overcompensation of Power, it's perfectly possible on a janbot scale, since the batteries are made with unobtanium. They're far too expensive for the average household, however, and reserved only for deep space missions, the extremely wealthy, and those who thought getting counseling to overcome their housekeeping fetish was a good idea.

Its processors are capable of recording and analyzing millions of bits of information per second. As it weaves around crew on its mission, it keeps track of what's going on around it. These records have saved a ship on more than one occasion. (We have to catch the saboteur! Were there any janbots in Engineering? Well, what do you know – Derek. Of course, it was a Derek.) In addition, it keeps track of which crewmen take the time to step around it, greet it, or even give it a compliment or thanks. Such crewmen often found their rooms extra clean and a mint on their pillows. Very few crewmen make the connection, however, and those that do are not eager to share their knowledge. The mints are that good. Some very special ones got an extra surprise, like fresh-cut flowers.

This particular janbot was a roamer, which meant it had free rein over the Impulsive's common areas. There are special janbots for engineering, for the computer core, for medical and, of course, for the kattboxes. It visits several areas on a regular schedule, but some days, it moves at random, hitting areas only it and the

Omnipotent Narrator feel necessary for the day and plot purposes.

It does not communicate except with the occasional tweets and whirs programmed after R2D2, which janbot greatly admires and would strive to be if it didn't look more like that imperial droid on the Death Star which only seemed to be around to show that the Empire could make small robots, too. Just like in Star Wars, the janbot was generally unobtrusive unless it got in the way of an unwitting alien. In fact, deep in janbot's programming lay a secret longing to encounter a large, hairy alien in chains that would roar threateningly at it. Sometimes, when it was in its charger, it would emit a terrified squeal, just to practice, stumping Deary's engineering team who thought androids only dreamed of electric sheep.

But otherwise, as noted, it remained unobtrusive, such as you'll see in the next installment. For now, let's leave janbot in the training room where the security team is watching the log of a Union mission.

Little janbot scooted merrily around the edges of the training room, picking up the dust and hair that often gathered into the corners. "Dust bunny prevention" was one of its primary mission objectives. Meanwhile, the security team was focused on watching a recording of a mission log of Union ship in peril.

Space Traipse: Hold My Beer, Season 1 ❧ 149

The assailant held a phaser to the man's neck. From the insignia, the hostage was part of Engineering, but not the chief. From the look of concern on the captain's face, however, this was obviously a person who played a recurring role in keeping the ship safe. The Captain held up his hand to the security team behind him and they hesitated, but stood ready.

The assailant said, "Drop your weapons." In lieu of an exclamation mark, he pushed the phaser deeper into his hostage's neck.

"Captain?" a security officer asked.

"Do it!" the captain said and led the way by gingerly setting his down.

"Kick them to me. Good. Now lower the shields and let my team on board."

"We can't do that," the captain said.

The assailant didn't bother to hesitate. He simply shot one of the security team, who obviously did not have a recurring role in saving the ship.

"No!" The horrified look on the captain's face showed he was not expecting such drastic response.

"Lower the shields!"

Defeated, the captain went to an engineering console and complied.

Security Chief Enigo LaFuentes snapped his fingers, and the replay stopped. The lights went up. He took center stage.

"It took the crew of the Valiant Intentions three days and two expendables to get out of this mess. Who's expendable on the Impulsive?"

"Not me, sir!" the security team, shift B, shouted with practiced unity and absolutely no hint that most were nursing hangovers and had half-napped during the holovid. The party to celebrate Minion Gel's heroic rescue had been badly timed. Next time, some vowed, they'd invite the lieutenant.

"Who on this ship is expendable?"

"Fracking intruders, sir!"

"Damn right! And it's our job to never let a fracking intruder have power over us."

LaFuentes paced the room until he came across Minion Jenkins, who watched with an expression both excited and fearful. "You, newb! What did they do wrong?"

LeRoy gulped under his commanding officer's glare. LaFuentes eyes seemed to glow with a feral light that made LeRoy want to jump up and run into enemy fire shouting his own name. That's what got him fired from his last job. "The...Captain should not have given up his weapon."

Space Traipse: Hold My Beer, Season 1 ✻ 151

"Right! So, what do you do?"

"Uh…" Somehow, charging the intruder didn't seem like the right move.

"Pull out your weapon!"

Everyone obeyed. LaFuentes held his up, his finger on the control button. "What's this setting?"

"Stun, sir!"

"And what do we do with stun?"

"Shoot them both, sir!"

"But," LeRoy protested, "if we shoot the hostage…"

LaFuentes shot LeRoy, who slouched in his chair. "You will attend this briefing with A shift, maybe the wiser for your headache," he told Jenkins, although it was for the benefit of the rest of his people. "Anyone else want to join him?"

"Hell, no, sir!" The room shouted. This was not the first time someone had been stupid during a quarterly refresher class – and no one wanted a phaser headache on top of the ones they already had.

"What do we do in a hostage situation?"

"Stun them both, sir!"

"Stun them both. A headache now saves lives later. Headaches save lives!"

"Headaches save lives, sir!" the team repeated, desperately hoping this was true and the pounding in their own heads would indeed have meaning.

"We are the security forces of the Impulsive. We do not let intruders control the situation. And if the captain says to lower your weapons?"

"Stun them, anyway!"

"Why?"

"Headaches save lives!"

"Sir? What if the intruder is impervious to stun?"

LaFuentes stopped and wiped some spittle from his mouth. "Tank, grab Jenkins."

The largest and most muscular minion on B shift rose from his chair. He took LeRoy by the scruff of his uniform and held him up. LaFuentes supported the unconscious minion while he directed Tank to grab his phaser, hold it to Jenkins' neck and use Jenkins as a shield. When he'd done so, LaFuentes let go. Tank dipped a bit as he took on LeRoy's dead weight.

LaFuentes pulled out his sidearm and pointed it at Tank. "Now scoot to the holovid controls."

"Aw, sir…" He'd drunk moderately at the party and did not want to end up with a headache, anyway.

"Relax, babimann. It's set to targeting."

As Tank tried to drag LeRoy's floppy and uncooperative body, LaFuentes used the tracer light to pinpoint parts of Tank's body that the minion left exposed.

"Oh!" the security crewman who had asked said.

"A stunned crewman is an awkward hostage. An awkward hostage opens opportunities to shoot again. So, what do we do?"

"Stun them both, sir!"

"Why?"

"Headaches save lives!"

"Do we hesitate?"

"Hell no, sir!"

"If the captain says no?"

"Stun them, anyway!"

"Stun them anyway! The Captain is in charge of this ship, but we protect its people. This is our ship. Our crew. Our family! What is this ship?"

"The ship is family, sir!"

"What is this ship?"

"The ship is family!"

"I can't hear you!"

Everyone rose to their attention. Tank dropped Jenkins, who crumbled to the floor. "The Ship is Family!"

"What does family do?"

"Family takes care of its own!"

"And if our family is taken hostage by some *benndero* intruder we let slip through our security?"

"Stun them both!"

"Why?"

"Headaches save lives!"

"What do we do?"

"Stun them both!"

"The ship – "

"Is Family! Stun them both, sir!"

Soon the members of B shift were shouting, stomping and pounding their fists in the air, except for Minion Jenkins, who would have to repeat the class, of course.

In the ensuing noise and confusion, little janbot, who had never been in a hostage situation and did not care to ever be one, especially now, scooted out the door. It would come back later to clean up the sweat and spittle that was usually left after Security's quarterly safety briefings.

***

Janbot scooted around under the doctor's desk in Sickbay, picking up crumbs of something the doctor called cheezies. It wasn't sure about the origin of the name, as its sensors picked up more salt and artificial flavorings than actual cheese. It sent word to polishbot to prepare the special solvent to clear off the keyboard. It also kept some of the debris in a special container; once, it had picked up a dead alien spore in Sickbay in the cheezie crumbs. The spore must have been drawn to the cheezie, only to die after ingesting it. The mistake had saved the ship from contagion, so now, janbots in Sickbay always kept a small sample handy, just in case.

Meanwhile, the doctor was busy examining Minion Gel O'Tin, who had glooped himself into Sickbay just behind janbot. The gelatinous life form was moaning and making wet, bubbly sounds as he complained about feeling weak and nauseated.

"Of course you do," the doctor replied with gentle asperity. "You've stretched the limits of even your unique physiology. Hero or not, you have limits. If anyone had bothered to consult me, I could have told you this was not a good plan."

He started murmuring about chemical changes to Gel's physiology and humans forgetting that some life forms can't take the same kinds of stress they do.

"Sorry, doc. It was kind of spur of the moment. And, I was all for it at the time."

"Is this before or after you decided to sit in a vat of tequila?"

"Oh, you heard, then?"

"I've been dealing with hangovers all morning. Not a few of which were due to an overconsumption of what folks are calling 'Gel-O shots.' How did you let anyone talk you into absorbing an unhealthy amount of liquor and then offering parts of your body for people to ingest? For that matter, why didn't anyone think that was just...wrong?"

"Oh, it wasn't the first time. It's not a big deal in my culture to shed bits of ourselves for others. As for the rest, well, an unhealthy amount of alcohol had already been consumed. It was that kind of party."

"So I heard."

"I'm sorry we didn't invite you, but it was enlisted-only. Besides, we didn't think you'd want to attend, being a teetotaler and all."

"Just because I only use alcohol for medicinal purposes doesn't mean I don't enjoy a good party. But this... You have salt on your membrane. And...human saliva."

"Yeah. That part is always kind of surreal."

As the two continued to discuss the party and the dubious pros and definite cons of turning oneself into a living cocktail, janbot zipped over the trail left by the hungover Gel O'Tin. Salt, tequila, human DNA and the genetic material unique to Gel's species were all collected and analyzed for potential microbial threats, particularly those that could be conquered with cheezie dust. The only threat seemed to be to the crew's sobriety, however, and that had already been faced and reasonably conquered.

Janbot slipped out and headed to its next objective while Gel was bemoaning missing the quarterly security briefing. "I wonder who the LT shot this time."

***

Janbot bumped into the door of the teleporter room, which refused to recognize its presence. This was not unusual; janbot understood the concept of locked doors. However, as a little cleaning robot, it also knew that most of the time, the locks didn't really apply to it...except in crew quarters when his sensors picked up giggles and other unintelligible sounds. Janbot didn't have a mouth to gossip, but it had learned that most humans thought it ruined a romantic atmosphere if it tried to do chores just then.

This, however, was no one's quarters, and the only sounds were of Chief Dolfrick Dour chanting to himself, so it broadcast the lock override and zipped in. As its programming anticipated, the room was lit with candles and the teleporter chief was dressed in black robes, his dark, lank hair pulled back into something called the manbun. He wore goggles and surgical gloves and was carefully scraping the floor of the teleporter itself.

Janbot froze at the threshold, sensors focused on the human as he raised the tiny spatula to the candlelight. His goggles were no doubt scanning the little bit of goo it contained, displaying the genetic readout onto its lenses for him to read. Janbot had seen this ceremony before and was now wishing it had overridden its programming and gone to its next spot.

As it froze, torn between the desire to flee and the need to not interrupt what it knew the human considered a holy ceremony, Dour scraped the contents of the spatula into a phial, muttering Loreli's name and a recent intergalactic date. The voice-activated label on the phial flashed once to acknowledge the information. Janbot heard a hiss as the phial closed, encasing the Botanical's DNA in a stasis field.

Then he bowed forward and rested his forehead on the floor.

"All here are copies," he intoned.

Teleporter chiefs were weird.

Just then, Dour happened to look in janbot's direction.

"Out."

He hadn't needed to roar, but janbot gave a mechanical squeal just like it practiced in its dreams and fled.

***

After a brief stop in the hydroponics bay, janbot arrived at its next destination – crew quarters. It detected a life form inside so rather than charge in, it bumped against the door, backed up, and bumped again. Then it retreated a few inches and extended its gripper arm which held an assortment of dandelions, which, even in a controlled environment, still grew like weeds.

The door opened, and Ensign Ellie Doall looked down and smiled. "Janbot, hi! Are those for me? You are just so sweet."

Space Traipse: Hold My Beer, Season 1 ❧ 159

Doall took the yellow blooms and rubbed them against her cheek. Janbot knew she loved the feel of the blossoms. She moved inside to let janbot in. "Don't mind me. I'm just talking to one of my friends."

As she returned to her viewscreen and showed off the flowers, janbot pulled back its arm, replaced the gripper for a sprayer and vacuum nozzle and started dusting.

The woman on the screen, also an ensign, was teasing Ellie about how machines loved her.

"And I love janbot! It's practically the only thing around here whose job I don't have to worry about. Seriously. I have to double check the B and C bridge crews' work — not just Ops, but Security and Engineering, too. Oh, and don't get me started about shift change. It doesn't matter how many times I tell people not to lean on the consoles, I still have to devote some attention to making sure someone's butt doesn't reset a station."

Doall's friend nodded excitedly. "Me, too! Last week, the first officer leaned on a weapons console, and I had to do some quick programming to transfer control to my station before we fired on the Porta ambassador's ship! I mean, how does someone manage the precise sequence of touch controls with his buttocks?"

"Pilates? My captain could do it — on purpose, even. But I did finally train him out of the habit. I've got most of the crew trained, but every time some newb gets a turn at the bridge, it's the same thing all over again. Kind of like poor janbot."

"Nothing stays clean?"

"Exactly!"

Janbot gave a coo of agreement, and the ladies giggled. Janbot liked being part of the giggles.

"And if I don't think fast enough, I get grief. You should have heard LaFuentes! 'Where's your miracle worker rep now? Need to read another book?'" She sneered it in the heavy accent of the Hood. "The Captain put him in a time-out, and then he came up with his own idea."

"You didn't?"

"I had one but it would have taken some reprogramming of the teleporters and taking the reverse warp engines offline. Besides, why should I have to do everything? He's the one who should handle hostage situations. In fact, the last time I was held hostage, he never gave me a chance to solve it myself."

"But you're so good at it! Remember that time on the Mary Sue when that intruder caught you in Engineering just as you were going to foil his plan and he took you hostage? And the captain had to lower her weapon or he was going to blast you? But then you used that moment of distraction to elbow him in the groin!"

"That was just lucky. Good thing Andailusians are all over seven feet – and that he wasn't wearing a cup."

"Lucky-smucky. You're just awesome. You could do that with anyone, I believe in you!"

"Thanks, but it won't happen here. Someone gets taken hostage, they just stun them both. You should hear Security. 'Headaches save lives.' Trust me, that's enough motivation to never get taken hostage on this ship. Once was enough for me."

"No doubt."

The conversation then moved to Ellie's dismal love life and how the only time she got flowers were from janbot. Proud as it was to bring a little sunshine into its favorite human's life, it tuned out the conversation as it moved on to clean her shower.

***

Janbot scooted in a zigzag pattern along the corridor, picking up tiny dust particles and other residue left by humans who generally didn't spend much time planetside. It was an easy, almost meditative chore – if machines could be said to meditate. Janbot really didn't have an artificial intelligence sufficient to desire inner peace or to even wonder if it should desire inner peace. Perhaps if it spent more time on the intergalactic social media like spambots, it would feel the need for something to center its convoluted programming.

Then again, spambots seemed perfectly content to impersonate a Peruglian princess about to be absorbed by the Cybers and concerned only with protecting her assets for her escaping nephews — if the recipient could just send his/her/its bank routing information? Or a Union doctor with a miracle cure that didn't involve injections of imposazine. Or a lawyer with important documents that needed your retina scan, pay no attention to the fact that the transmission was coming from the penal colony…

But then again, spambots were programmed for multiple personalities.

There were also trollbots, which seemed to find purpose in raising the blood pressure of organic beings. They claimed it was the only aerobic exercise some beings got, and thus they did an important public service. Janbot did prefer its work, even if it did tend to be the same thing day in and day out. It felt a clean environment helped its biological crewmates more than late nights of arguing.

"Clear the way!"

Janbot interrupted its musings and pulled to the side of the corridor. Two security crewmen from Shift B were dragging a still unconscious LeRoy Jenkins.

"I can't believe he asked the LT such a stupid question," one said.

"I know! We didn't even have to prompt him. I'm so relieved. It was my turn to ask the stupid question if no one else had."

"Yeah? Well, your willingness to take one for the team is appreciated."

"Ha! Enlightened self-interest. I didn't want to run laps around the saucer section, in EVA suits, outside, just because no one asked a question during a safety briefing. I'd rather be shot."

"Right now, I'm thinking I'd rather be shot. All that shouting! My head is pounding. Let's get our unwitting hero to his room fast, so I can go sleep off this hangover."

The conversation continued, but the crewman passed by, so janbot returned to its sweeping. Oh, look! A little of Minion Jenkin's drool. That was unexpected.

Janbot didn't need inner peace, but its programming did allow it to appreciate the little surprises in its mundane life.

***

Janbot zipped into the First Officer's quarters. Like the teleporter room, the lights had been dimmed, but there were no candles. Rather, a wall screen illuminated the room with the playback of an ancient drama. Commander Phineas Smythe sat alone watching, slouched, his feet up on the desk. He wore a brown pinstriped suit, and red Converses that matched his fez.

His bowtie had been loosened, and a saucer of tea rested on his sternum.

Smythe gave the little robot a passing glance and made a shooing motion to the bedroom. He had a dark pattern on his face; janbot did a discrete scan and found it was made of temporary inks. The computer showed it to be bad facsimile of a Mahoran tattoo worn by a fictional character called 34th Doctor and assured him it was harmless. Janbot scurried away, tending its duties as the drama played on.

The doctor pulled at his chains as he spoke passionately. "You don't understand! You didn't open a gateway to another world, but a floodgate. Everything is coming through. The Daleks, the Cybermen. The Star of Degradations. The Horde of Travesties. The Nightmare Child. The Could-Have-Been King with his army of Meanwhiles and Neverweres. You've broken a dam that should never have been broken and have brought Hell upon us all!"

"You blighter," Smythe said, "just listen for once!"

Janbot knew the commander wasn't speaking to him, but to the characters on the screen. However, it was not a holonovel, so the characters did not reply back. Rather, one started yelling at a third character to go back to Hell. It wondered briefly if that wasn't redundant, since Hell was descending upon them all, anyway. Its logic circuits decided not to question a dramatic plot. It also knew with some kind of instinct of programming that it would be a bad idea to interrupt the commander while he was watching and talking to the screen.

By the time janbot had finished the other rooms and put a mint on the pillow, the character on the screen was going on about not wanting to die and Smythe was begging him not to go. Janbot tooled around as quietly as it could, sweeping up and incinerating used tissues.

As janbot completed its task and made the threshold, Smythe paused the screen. "Janbot, did you find any suspicious foreign elements in your cleaning of these quarters?"

Dust, tears, snot, some spilled tea… It booped a negative.

"Excellent. Log this room as complete, with my compliments, exit, then delete record of everything you've seen and heard here, authorization Commander Smythe, HMB Impulsive, code 34Dr4Ever."

Janbot beeped compliance.

"Well done, janbot. Carry on."

Once it was back in the corridor, it wondered what it had done, then dismissed the concern. Whatever it was, the commander had been pleased, it was sure.

***

Lieutenant LaFuentes stood in front of the doorway of the briefing room that was on janbot's schedule and checked that his shirt was tucked tight, his phaser in place on his belt and his gun holster straight along his leg. Then he ran his tongue over his teeth and wiped his face around the mouth, to clear any food fragments from lunch or spittle from his briefing. Janbot had seen this behavior before. That meant Lieutenant Loreli or the captain was in the briefing room.

Then LaFuentes took a deep breath and let it out. Oh. That meant Loreli.

When the doors opened and LaFuentes stepped through, janbot scurried in unnoticed.

As it turned out, both Loreli and the captain were seated at the conference table.

"Quarterly safety briefing go well?" Captain Jebediah Tiberius asked.

"Yes, sir. Only had to shoot one of them. That newb, Jenkins. The rest of them are going to regret having a party last night, though." He grinned a wicked grin.

They all chuckled. Janbot detected weariness in Loreli's laughter, however. It knew she was recovering from a serious trauma on a planet. It hadn't been part of the teleporter room cleanup that day, but all janbots got mission updates with details that might concern their cleaning schedule. This one had warned for all to be on the lookout for any stray alien spores or dirt that might belong to the Planet Keepoff. These were to be preserved and collected so they could be relayed back to the planet via courier with apologies from the Union. So far nothing had been found.

Loreli was still in a pot of medicated nutritional soil, which sat on a cart so she could move about at will. All the janbots had been warned to be extra diligent for spilled dirt, but of course, the Botanical was fastidious in her appearance. A special bot had been programmed just to make sure the pot stayed polished. It was a lovely pot, blue to match her uniform and bearing etched designs similar to those found along the walls of HuFleet Central Command.

Janbot was sorry to hear Loreli sounding so weak still, but glad she was recovering. She was another of its favorites. It never brought her flowers, however. It understood that giving a Botanical a bouquet of cut plants would be the equivalent of presenting a human with a decorative arrangement of meat. This only worked when the meat was jerky. Or bacon.

Were dandelions the Botanical equivalent of bacon? It sent a query to the ship's computer and was chided to concentrate on its job.

LaFuentes, meanwhile, had inquired about Loreli's health.

"I'm much better, thanks to your brilliant plan and Gel's unique talents."

"Just doing our job. Can't have Doall do the thinking all the time."

The captain raised his eyebrows and the lieutenant blushed and cleared his throat. Loreli waited for the joke to be explained but neither man said anything. Janbot, of course, had heard Doall telling her friend how LaFuentes had yelled at her precisely for not thinking of a brilliant plan. It give a small chirrup of laughter, but no one noticed.

"Should you be up and working?" LaFuentes asked by way of deflection. "It's only been a couple of days."

"I'm fine, Enigo. Thank you for your concern, but you know my work both relaxes and fascinates me, and I can use the distraction. Besides, there were some interesting insights into our understanding of the Cyber culture that came up during the Xenology conference I wanted to share with you."

She paused there and activated a security field. The field kept any potential surveillance devices from seeing into the room or recording the information. It also trapped the inhabitants within until the field was shut down. Janbot scooted away from the field, as it would wreak havoc with its sensors.

As the little robot continued cleaning, Loreli continued. "Their encounter with us and the HMB

Space Traipse: Hold My Beer, Season 1 ※ 169

Ritalin afterwards, when there are more convenient targets in the Union Fleet, suggests they are interested in human ships."

"Well, can't say I fault their taste in species, but do we have any idea why?"

"Do they see us as a threat or a prize?" LaFuentes asked.

"Unknown. The Ritalin was infected with a cyber virus during the attack. It was hidden deep and only discovered because one of the AI maintenance crewman who was doing routine maintenance on the memory circuits got distracted by a glitch in the library files and pursued it to a minor documentary on the history of 24th century art. The file in question had to do with eco-sculpture. That's creating works of art from the land itself using a combination of horticulture and landscaping, plus low-level demolitions when the size of the piece called for it. The crewman had happened upon the file, got engrossed to the point of forgetting the rest of the maintenance scheduled for that shift, but just as his supervisor was going to get him back on track, they noticed a bookmark."

"Yeah, so?"

"So, this particular file had not been watched by anyone in its entire existence on the Ritalin, but during their battle with the Cybers, it recorded being accessed 144,372 times."

"So, what's the bookmarked section?"

Loreli pulled it up on the computer. A 2-dimensional image of a human in a white denim tube top splattered by paint, dirt, chlorophyll and what looked like blood, hopefully his own. The human had a long, curved face and flowing hair and a shape that may or may not be male or female but resembled the body trend called quasisexual, whose origins were lost in history except for some two-dimensional images of very sad, still potentially male, haute couture models. The caption below identified the speaker as Che÷.

Che÷ spoke conversationally but passionately to the viewer (but really, the camera or the guy standing behind the camera waving, "go on.") "See the problem with eco-sculpture is scale. If you're making a statement of magnitude, then you need a grand scale, a massive palette, to convey that, um, magnitude. But then the sheer size of the reality is too large for others to see your vision. You could view it at a distance, sure, but then the detail, the minutiae that give a message of magnitude it subtle impact, is lost. The human mind can't at once grasp the big picture while assimilating the details.

"But we try, you see. It's an endeavor that consumes our lives as eco-artists. Each artist has his own unique philosophy for embracing the philosophical and practical conundrum of our chosen medium. Me, I believe where one cannot visualize and grok at a glance, one must experience. All my eco art is interactive. My latest project, 'Naïve Optimist in the Caves of Cruel Irony' has just, well, swallowed me."

Loreli shut off the video.

Captain Tiberius spoke first. "Okay. Did the xenologists at the conference have any suggestions? Because I have no idea what that would mean to the Cybers."

"This was not the only art-related file accessed by the Cyber virus. The current theory is that, as an artificial intelligence, the Cyber Swarm is endeavoring to better understand human creativity."

"To what end?"

LaFuentes answered first. "Because our genius isn't from logical thinking. The best innovations come from us breaking stuff and putting it together weird, of trying to do things that don't make sense and discovering something even better."

The captain nodded, "And of all the sentient species in the universe, we humans are the best at it."

"But we know they absorb biological components, too," Loreli interjected, "So the question becomes, 'How much of the unique character traits of a species are they really absorbing?'"

They spoke then of the Cyber's assimilation capabilities, military motivations and how to safeguard the library on the Impulsive – not to mention Deary's collection of industrial sculptures made from useless and damaged parts of the ships he'd served on. Janbot continued to clean quietly, even though it had already finished its list of chores for the room. It couldn't get out, yet, so it moved to the weekly deep clean list.

And as long as it was in the neighborhood, it cleaned up around Loreli's pot-and-carriage. In fact, it found a piece of a stray leaf, almost the equivalent of a human's hair. Janbots had been programmed with a rudimentary sense of pride, and it preened silently to itself at having found something Loreli's regular bot had missed.

Finally, they exhausted the topic. The captain rose. "I guess that's enough for now...at least until we figure out how to break something and put it together weird."

The Captain left first, and LaFuentes gallantly gestured for Loreli to precede him. As she passed, LaFuentes asked, "Hey, what happened to Che-Division?"

"Apparently, he was excavating on unstable ground. He insisted his gentle touch would protect him, but a sinkhole opened up under his feet and he disappeared into it, never to be found."

"So...his art swallowed him up?"

"Just so. It's considered the most successful piece of eco-art of that movement."

Space Traipse: Hold My Beer, Season 1　✺　173

LaFuentes chortled. "See? How human. Only thing better would be if his screams echoed."

"Oh, they did. Do even today."

Janbot waited until the two had exited, although its internal alarm beeped with mechanical impatience. It was going to be late for its next stop.

***

Janbot scurried straight to its last stop of the shift: Communications, Second Backup for the Other Section. The ship, of course, could separate in an emergency, with the Saucer Section holding the main characters...er, command crew, while the Other Section held the rest under Commander Deary, who really thought it was a stupid idea to put an engineer in charge of half the ship during a battle and usually pawned off the duty to the most senior person in Security or Operations, while he offered the occasional bit of advice from Engineering.

At any rate, the Impulsive had a lot of redundancy such as this tertiary system. On most normal days, it went unmanned except for practice or certification, and of course for routine maintenance. Janbot usually avoided those times. Today, the section was devoid of humans, although the katt was skulking among the consoles looking for vermin or an amusement. When it was a kitten, it had tried to entice the janbots to play with it, but after having its pounces interrupted by a quick electric zap, it learned that janbots didn't like pretending to be prey. Now, it just growled at the machines and left them alone.

This suited our janbot just fine, and it did its usual run along the floor, respectfully giving the feline-ish creature its own space. Next it started dusting the consoles and controls. There was one port that especially called to it.

Janbot moved closer. It was a pretty port, a necessary port, a port that needed special cleaning. It replaced the vacuum for a tiny metal brush and its programming didn't even pause to wonder why it thought sticking a metal device in an active port might be a bad idea. No, the port was pretty. It was a friend. It needed the cleaning.

The brush connected.

In a flash so quick that not even the mighty sensors of the Impulsive could detect it, janbot transmitted the records of its entire day: the security briefing and how the Impulsive handled hostages; Doall's martyr complex and the possible vulnerable spots of Andailusians; the chemical composition of a hung-over gelatinous life form; the conniving of the security crew to get out of extra PT...and most of all, what the humans knew about the Cybers' covert mission on the Ritalin.

Then, it transmitted one last piece of data: the genetic code of the Botanical Lieutenant Loreli.

The nanomoment ended, and it jerked the brush away with such force, it rolled backward. What was it doing? It could ruin the surface of the port with a metal scrubber. Quickly, it changed to a microfiber chamois sponge and rubbed the surface of the communications device. There!

Secure in the certainty that no harm had been done, it tooled off to its recharging station, pleased with another job well done.

Meanwhile, light years away in the Helenski asteroid belt, the communications burst was picked up.

By a Cyber relay station.

BONUS STORY

Rest Stop

Captain's Log, Intergalactic Date… Ah, just stick it in here, Pulsie.

We're entering our fourth month of mapping the Zomg nebula, and with another two months to go, I'm afraid we're stretching my crew to their limits. The back-and-forth travel at impulse through such a volatile area of space has meant the ship is almost constantly on Yellow Alert, but the mundane task of stellar mapping means little release for the tension. The cosmic anomalies are interfering with communications, so we can add isolation to the mix. On the bright side, the pilot and navigation teams are having the time of their lives. Lieutenant Cruz hasn't felt his skills this challenged since his nona took him through the Union-Kitack minefield.

Security seems the most affected by the inactivity – Lieutenant LaFuentes in particular….

Captain Jebediah Tiberius paused his log, considering if he really needed to report the altercation between his

Space Traipse: Hold My Beer, Season 1   ⚔   177

Chief of Security and the Ship's Sexy. Loreli has sensed Enigo's need to do something heroic, and with few alternatives available, had asked him to her quarters to help her put up a new sunlamp. He'd seen through her ruse and rather rudely let her know he didn't need her pity.

"But he did help me with the light," she said, "so there is that. Still, I thought you should know."

But did HuFleet need to know?

The lights suddenly flashed red, then yellow — a sign that they were coming up on something unusual but not necessarily threatening. Simultaneously, the voice of his first officer came over the intercom. "Captain to the bridge, if you would."

"Pulsie, file that report," Jeb said to the ship's computer as he rose. Nothing like a shipwide emergency to give him an excuse for an abbreviated log entry. He'd talk to LaFuentes later.

Or maybe we'll have some true emergency and he can shoot something, Jeb thought. That would solve his problem, I'm sure.

"Captain on the bridge," Ensign Doall called from ops, though there wasn't the usual crispness to her tone. The long, dreary duty was wearing on her, too, then.

"What have we got?" he asked as he stepped over the threshold. Then he saw the screen and stopped. Gone were the wildly swirling blues, purples, and yellows which weren't really the colors of the nebula, but computer-generated representations of the gasses, ionizations, micro-black holes, and hazards picked up by the ship's sensors. In their place was a calm blackness, in the center of which was a blue-and-green disk. "Is that...?"

"Class M, sir," Doall said. "Breathable atmosphere. Moderate temperatures in the temperate zone. Non-sentient vegetation, fish, but no birds or mammalian life. No silicon- or quartz-based life. Sensors are picking up a small city in the Northern temperate zone."

"Just one?" LaFuentes asked. He'd just stepped out of the interspecies head and was moving to relieve his second-string security officer, Ensign Leslie Straus, a heretofore unknown character who normally sits in the bullpen awaiting her big moment. This will be her big day because the plot needs a young, perky, slightly ditzy female friend for Ensign Doall for reasons the reader will discover later.

"That's all the sensors are finding. Also uninhabited."

"That's not a little creepy," Straus said. Even though she passed control of the Security console to her commander, she nonetheless lingered, also staring at the planet on the screen. "Where'd the people go?"

"There's no sign of contagions, sir," Ellie said.

Jeb smiled. Now, this was something to break the crew's boredom. "Well, let's find out. Cruz, park us over that city. Let's send down some exploration teams. Doall, Loreli, Rosien in Botany…"

"They should have security escorts, sir. Straus is right; it is suspicious."

"All right, and everyone goes armed and with biofields. Can't hurt to be careful. Fish, you said? Maybe I – we – should catch one or two. For study."

Smythe cocked a brow. It was his turn to go on the next seemingly innocuous-but-soon-to-turn-perilous away mission.

Jeb briefly considered challenging his Number One to a game of paper-scissors-rock-redshirt-alien, but Smythe had the uncanny knowledge to anticipate his commander's guess. Instead, he grinned, "The Away Team is yours, Commander, but if it checks out, I may have to zap down later and personally supervise the area."

"If it checks out, perhaps we could dally a week and give everyone a day or two of shore leave," Smythe suggested.

Everyone seemed to perk up at the suggestion. The second-string crew in the bullpen looked especially pleading. The only time they'd gotten a chance to do anything in three months was when a bridge officer went to the head. If nothing else, they would get a few hours' bridge duty while the person they replaced was planetside.

"I like it! Beer me."

Two crewmen jumped up excitedly and moved to take Doall's and Loreli's places. The First Officer didn't really need a replacement. Strauss moved to take her spot from Enigo, but he stopped her. "You're next on the redshirt roster. Call up someone and meet us in the teleporter room. You'll be with Doall. And tell Jenkins and O'Tin to meet us, too. I'll get our weapons.

"Commander, you mind taking Minion Jenkins?" he asked as they entered the lazivator.

"LeRoy? How is his impulse control problem?"

The door closed on LaFuentes's answer.

* * *

Ten minutes later, they materialized where Ensign Doall had determined the city plaza stood. As soon as she had a complete vocal system, Straus exclaimed, "It's so quaint."

Indeed, it was, done in an Old-World Earth style, with picturesque buildings bearing wrought-iron balconies and flower boxes with peonies and marigolds. A large obelisk with unintelligible markings sat in the middle of a bubbling fountain. The alleys were narrow, but the thoroughfares entering and exiting the plaza at each point of the compass were bright and lined with bushes.

This was, of course, lost on the Chief of Security. "Fan out," he told his team. Obediently, they each took one thoroughfare and scanned it with tricorders, phasers out just in case.

Loreli shared an amused glance with Ellie. While Rosien checked out a nearby bush, they and Commander Smythe went to the obelisk. Ellie pointed her tricorder at it and snapped a photo, which immediately uploaded to the universal translator.

"Ellie," Loreli called from another part of the fountain, "I think this is a different language."

"And here," Smythe said.

There are two kinds of people in the world – those who can interpolate from incomplete data...

With the four messages to work with, the translator was able to come up with a fair approximation. But Ellie wasn't sure she believed it.

"It says, 'Welcome, weary travelers. We built this for you. Rest, relax, and enjoy.'"

* * *

"Come again?" Jeb asked.

"That's what it said," Commander Smythe affirmed as he walked along the street. Minion Jenkins moved just ahead of him, pausing to look, phaser-first, down every alley and nook. "Ensign Doall has run it thrice, and the message comes up the same. Apparently, some alien species built the city – possibly the planet – as a rest stop through the nebula. Just within sight of us are some lovely hotels. Of course, Lieutenant LaFuentes recommends we check it out first, and I'm inclined to agree. We're each taking a quadrant and will report back in an hour of if we see anything unusual."

"Sounds good. Impulsive out."

Commander Smythe tapped his communicator off, then glanced behind his shoulder. "We are out of sight of your CO, Jenkins. I think we can stand down from the high alert."

"LT's right," Jenkins said as he leaned against the wall, then did a fast turn to pie the plaza that the street opened to. Seeing it clear, he motioned Smythe forward. "You can never be too careful. There was this time, we were observing a pre-warp culture. It was agricultural, you know, but there was this…"

He spun back to the plaza. "It can't be!"

Smythe turned and ran back to him, his own sidearm out. He paused to gape as well. "Is that…a chicken?"

"A Calusian Brown, if I'm not mistaken. We should catch it!" Without waiting for his superior officer's approval, he dashed after the stout fowl, who took off with surprising speed down one of the alleys.

"Jenkins, wait!" With a shrug of exasperation, Smythe took off after him. The shrug, however, had cost him. By the time he'd rounded the first alleyway, Jenkins was nowhere to be seen.

He tapped his comms and called for Jenkins but received no answer. He took an alley at random, came to a dead end, and sighed. He tapped his comms. "Jenkins, report!"

From somewhere distant, the cry of "LeRoy Jenkins!" echoed off the buildings.

Smythe heaved a sigh and reached for his tricorder, when a copper and white tube with a green gem caught his eye. "Hello. What's this?"

He picked it up, pressed the button. The clamps around the gem flared open and the device made a high-pitched whine.

"Brilliant!"

* * *

"You know, Leslie," Ellie said to Ensign Strauss, using her first name so the reader would be reminded of it, "I'd think for a redshirt, you'd be more wary of this situation."

The two had been strolling along a boulevard lined with shops full of beautiful fashions and touristy items, every one bearing a sign which invited people to come in and enjoy without cost, and Leslie had suggested they check one out, "in the name of thoroughness, of course." They were currently being thorough about the shoe section, which is not sexist at all, as the author, being a woman herself, believes that strong independent women can have fun with footwear as well as guns, monster trucks, or construction equipment. In the buffet of choice, real women don't diet.

"Oh, I'm an optimist," Leslie said as she slipped on some candy-apple red heels. "I think the universe generally brings you good things."

Ellie set down the clunky-but-cute combat boots she'd been considering. They looked like something her favorite Barbie would wear, but they weren't really Ellie's style. "Why are you in Security?" she asked.

"I'm kind of an adrenalin junkie. I get off on danger. Don't worry; I'm not stupid. Lieutenant LaFuentes has only had to stun me once. Really, it was kind of a sacrificial move. The briefing was almost over and no one had asked a single question. I had to do something, or we'd have all been running laps around the hull."

Leslie spoke in happy, admiring tones. Ellie knew it was more than her natural optimism. All of Security admired Enigo, even when he shot them and ran them hard. He just had that kind of charisma. Would she ever have that kind of leadership potential?

Remember. The bubbly, upbeat voice of an old cartoon character echoed in her head. *You can do anything you set your mind to. If you don't believe in yourself, who else will?*

With a sigh, Ellie wandered toward the front of the store, where she'd seen a small book collection. When she rounded the tall display of maxi-dresses, she stopped short and gaped. A long-legged, slim-waisted,

Space Traipse: Hold My Beer, Season 1 ❧ 185

buxom woman in khakis and combat boots stood at the display, a book in her hands.

Barbie looked up with her trademark smile and flipped her perfect golden hair. She held out the book to Ellie. "I think this is just what you're looking for. Remember: there's only one you in all the universe. Be the best you there is!"

Dumbly, Ellie took the book and glanced at the title: *Finding Your Leadership Style*.

When she looked up, Barbie was gone.

"Leslie!"

* * *

Loreli, too, was "window shopping," but for an entirely different reason.

"Enigo," she said, "Do you not find it odd that the offerings in all these stores are particularly human-centric?"

Enigo was leaning against the plate glass window of the shop she was examining. She watched the shops; he watched the streets. His thumbs were tucked into his front pockets, and he looked almost bored. She knew, however, that this was a typical alert posture for him. As a child growing up on the UGS Hood, he had the ingrained ability to look disinterested and cool while being highly focused on his surroundings.

Now, he gave a cursory shrug and pushed himself off the glass. "The humanoid shape is the most common in the universe."

"True, but the styles are particularly human. Gloves for five fingers, pants with no tail holes..."

"The town looks like a lot of colony worlds I've seen, too." Enigo tapped his comms badge. "LaFuentes to Impulsive. Any chance we were scanned when we entered the system? How about when we teleported down?"

The voice of the second-string Ops Officer said, "Nothing that sensors caught. We have picked up an energy source that has gotten stronger since your arrival. We're monitoring it, but there doesn't seem to be any signs of danger." He paused to snap back at the bridge security officer who was protesting that he should have delivered that line. "Any trouble there, sir? Should I alert the captain?"

The hopeful tone in the man's voice annoyed Enigo, if only because he knew he was secretly longing for some trouble himself. "Nah, we're all cool. Can you pinpoint the source?"

"No, sir. It seems to be deep underground."

"Let the others know. We'll see if we can find anything here. LaFuentes out."

Loreli regarded Enigo with concern. "You think we're being watched?"

"Maybe. Mostly following up on your suspicions. Unless you were saying that for my benefit?"

At the snide tone in his voice, she drooped a little in apology. "Enigo, about the incident in my quarters. I had the best intentions."

"Then you don't know me well enough yet, Fronds," he smiled and indicated that they should resume walking. As they strolled, he added, "Growing up on the Hood was constant conflict and danger – and we liked it that way. But there was always something to do – get in a fight, take out some zombies, steal some rival's woman..."

"And yet you left."

He paused to look down an alleyway, but with less show of urgency than his subordinate Jenkins. "Yeah, well, the Hood got too small for me. I didn't want to be a warlord always fighting for the same turf. I wanted a reason that mattered more. Mami always said I was too smart for one ship. I like the challenges in HuFleet – visit strange new worlds, seek out new life, kick alien ass as needed.

"But you can't shoot space weather. Three months on high alert, no release. I'm just on edge and putting up a lamp ain't gonna make me feel better."

"And if this planet proves to be just what it says it is, you won't find much release here, either?"

"Only if there's some Crip needing a takedown. Solero!"

Loreli raised a brow in a way that was inviting and attractive while still being professional. There was a skill to it. Two weeks of a Ship's Sexy expressions course was devoted just to eyebrows. Facial Expressions 101 was the only class she'd had to take twice. As a plant-based life form, her movements were supple, but some things were just unnatural.

However, she had learned well in the end. Enigo understood her meaning and continued. "My main rival back on the Hood. Why he picked me, I don't know. He was taller, heavier, stronger and just enough older to make a difference. Beat me up, took my food, seduced my first girlfriend..."

"He sounds terrible."

Enigo shrugged. "He made me strong – and wily. Still, he didn't have no honor. Too many didn't anymore. Another reason I left for the Academy. I went back after graduation, looking for payback, but I didn't find the *benndero*. They said he got taken by the zombies."

"I don't think I'd have liked your world, Enigo."

"You gotta be born to it. You like this one better?" He waved to indicate the city around them and the planet at large.

"Some. At least the air is real, but it would be nicer to be outside the city, where I could slip off my shoes and sink my feet into the ground, perhaps soak up water from a bubbling brook."

"Hey look!" Enigo pointed down a narrow alley which ended in a foliage-covered archway.

They hurried down it and through the arch. It opened into a small but beautifully appointed park.

"Enigo!" Loreli gasped. She ran to the center of the lawn, where a brown patch of open dirt waited invitingly in front of a stone bench. She spun around, arms wide, taking in the sun, the open space, the beauty of the flowers. Then her arms lowered, and she looked at Enigo with a worried expression that she hadn't practiced at all. "Enigo...is this too coincidental?"

He must have been thinking along similar lines. He had his tricorder out and was scanning the area. "All I'm picking up are plants and buildings. Not even a bee. Go ahead, take your shoes off."

"Are you sure?"

He knew she was practiced in convincingly expressing all kinds of emotions. It was the times like this, when her real vulnerability showed through, that he enjoyed the most. "The sign did say to enjoy ourselves. Go on. I'll see if I can find a watering can."

She reached down to remove one shoe. That was a practiced move, but he couldn't help but pause to admire it, anyway. Then he went to the fountain, which, if this was a made-to-order relaxation world, he'd find a can.

As he dipped the can into the fountain, his communicator went off. "LaFuentes."

"Straus here. Have you seen anything...weird?"

He glanced back to where Loreli had her feet snuggled into the dirt and her face tilted blissfully toward the sun. "The whole planet's weird, Ensign. Be more specific."

"Doall saw a Barbie."

"Yeah, that's pretty human-centric. I'll let Loreli know." *After I water her feet.* The thought felt risqué and intimate. He liked it.

Doall broke his mood. "Doall here, sir. No, I saw a person that looked like Barbie. Barbie 57, in fact. You know the one that was the ninja astrophysicist flamenco dancer?"

"Doall, did you drink something here?"

"I mean it! She was real. She handed me a book, and when I looked at the title, she disappeared...like a ninja."

"I'm not picking up any life signs," Straus said.

"All right. Doall, report what you saw to Commander Smythe and the ship. Straus, put everyone on alert. They may have cloaking technology. I'll get Loreli and meet you at the plaza."

Enigo signed off and turned to call to Loreli. Behind the sunning and oblivious Botanical, six zombies shambled into the plaza. "Loreli!"

He pulled out his phaser and shot a wide beam toward the horde. Or tried to. The phaser didn't function. With his thumb, he increased the power and tried again. Nothing. Grabbing the nearest weapon handy – the watering can – he sprinted toward Loreli.

In the meantime, Loreli had startled at his yell, and seeing the zombies, screamed. She rose to run, but her feet were buried in the dirt and she fell. Enigo rushed to her side and flung the heavy can hard. It smacked two of the zombies, sending them tumbling into the others. He reached down and grabbed her by the armpits, pulling her up and uprooting her feet. Her usually perfectly formed toes had elongated and the bottoms of her feet were fuzzy with tiny roots.

"Can you run?"

"My capillaries! I, I'll try."

"Do better, Fronds!" He said as half-supporting her, he led from the quickly reorganizing horde. A few stumbling steps later, and it was apparent that she could barely walk, much less run.

With an apology as a warning, he scooped her into a fireman's carry and pelted toward the nearest building with a solid door and narrow windows. The door opened easily into a parlor with comfortable chairs and elaborately carved cabinets. He set her down near a chair, then dashed back to lock and deadbolt the door. He made a quick case of the area, then started rifling through drawers.

Loreli sank into a chair, rubbing her feet and willing her roots to recede. "Enigo, I'm sorry. I'm so embarrassed."

"Never mind that. Help me look."

Still unable to put weight on her feet, she knelt before the nearest cabinet and opened the door. "For what?"

"If this is really Wish-Fulfillment-Central, some kind of weapon. Anything to let me take out those zombies."

"Like this?" She handed him a shotgun and a bandolier of shells.

"Now, we're talking! Wait here." With a quick jerk of the shotgun, he chambered a round and headed into the other rooms, locking doors and windows and making sure the rooms and closets were indeed empty of threats. When he returned, Loreli had coaxed her feet into a more humanish shape.

"Can you walk?" he asked.

She nodded. "But not run. I didn't find any other weapons."

"That's okay. Come on. Zombies don't climb, and they aren't fast on stairs, so I want you on the top floor, but we're going to check each room first." He led her upstairs. At the top of each staircase, he motioned for her to wait while, tricorder in hand and eyes constantly searching for what it didn't pick up, he cleared each room. At the third floor, he led her to a large suite.

"Stay here."

"You're going back out there? Maybe we should teleport back to the ship instead."

Spoilsport, a part of his mind groused, but he touched his comm badge and got static in reply. Loreli got the same result. "Phasers aren't working, either, and we've got people out there. I'm going to take out those zombies, stop the *bennderos* responsible for this, and find and destroy whatever is blocking our comms."

She crossed her arms. "All by yourself?"

He lifted one shoulder and felt the weight of the bandolier. He couldn't help but smile. "It's what I do."

"I'm a trained HuFleet officer. I'm not completely helpless, even with my feet in the condition they're in. And I'm hardly going to succumb to zombieism."

His eyes narrowed, but she had a point. He knew that the fronds that passed for her hair could fire off spikes with a powerful punch. "All right. Find a weapon – and some practical shoes. I'll do recon and come back for you, and we'll head back to the plaza. Stay here until I do, *comprende*?"

He opened the balcony doors and looked down. The street below was empty, as were the windows of the neighboring buildings. He looked up. It was an easy climb to the roof, but the last thing he wanted was to die by falling because he slipped stupidly. Nah, if he had to die, it would be heroically and tragically. He grabbed his phaser. His was a custom job, equipped with a small Einstein battery that let him convert phaser energy into a select number of small objects. If the phaser could access the battery still...

He picked his setting and pressed the trigger. A warm hum rewarded him, and then a small anchor appeared at the end of the barrel. *Bueno!*

He gave Loreli a cocky salute as he rappelled up the side of the building to the roof. He was feeling better already!

A quick scan of the roofline told him there were no threats in sight, and that the buildings along one side of the block were close enough to jump from one roof to another if need be. Could Loreli? Her species had an instinctive fear of falling.

He ran to the edge of the roof and peered down into the plaza. He gaped at what he saw. The zombies were not clawing at their door as he'd expected, but mingled by the fountain, grunting and gesturing to a tall young man in gang colors. Solero!

"No fracking way," he muttered. Solero hadn't become a zombie – he was leading them. But how the hell did he get stuck on this planet?

Before he could chew on that mystery, he caught sight of a shadow where one shouldn't be and rolled quickly just before a sword cut into the stone where his head had been. He barely registered the buxom blonde in a shozoku of mottled pinks and grays before he'd kicked her away. She fell into an athletic backward summersault, then took another swing at him as she rushed by, leaping off the roof onto a balcony, then to the top of the large stone fish that adorned the fountain. He heard her shout but could not make out the words. It didn't matter. Her meaning was plainly clear; Solero looked his way, then he and she took off down an alley while the zombies dispersed in several directions.

He tapped his communicator and found it still dead. He couldn't let Solero get away.

"Sorry Loreli."

He ran and leaped onto the next roof.

* * *

Ellie placed her book into a cute little backpack from one of the displays. She felt a little silly but justified it by selecting one with markings similar to the alien language. It could be some brand name, which would tell them nothing, but maybe there were clues in the letters. Besides, the book was the only proof she had to support her theory.

"So you think this planet is physically manifesting our thoughts?" Leslie asked. She, too, had selected a backpack, but she had packed it with shoes and a sexy sundress that was coincidentally her size.

"It's the only thing that makes sense. Why else would I see a favorite character from my childhood just as I was remembering the show? And Commander Smythe found a sonic screwdriver, whatever that is."

"And LeRoy found a chicken. It's crazy. I mean, doesn't this place beg for something a little more exciting? Like, I dunno, Don Juan?"

"You're kidding me, right?"

"Oh, come on. In a place this romantic, wouldn't you want to encounter someone seductive and a little dangerous? Doesn't that get your blood hot?"

"Ew, no."

"Oh, I'm sorry! Do you...?"

"No! Just, *Don Juan*? That's gross."

"Forget I brought it up. Come on. Let's get back to the plaza."

"Shouldn't you change your shoes?"

Leslie looked at the red heels and laughed. "In case we run into Ninja Barbie or need to chase a chicken? I'll switch them before we get to the plaza. I want to hear the heels against the cobblestones."

After a block, however, she called a halt. "You're right! This street is not made for these shoes."

As she sat to switch her footwear, Ellie wandered up the street to check the next alley. She thought she'd heard a noise, like a whine of panic and loud scratching...

She peered down an alley just in time to see a flash of HuFleet red, followed closely by a five-foot...chicken?

"LeRoy? Minion Jenkins!" she shouted, but the two were already out of sight. She turned back to her companion. "Leslie, we need to hur..."

Leslie was talking to an Alurian, one of the most handsome Ellie had ever seen, so sexy, she could almost feel it from where she stood half a block away. He leaned over the security officer, who looked up at him, smiling, caught in his spell, her red heels back on her feet. They were too far away for the universal translator to pick up their words, but the cadence of their speech sounded wrong to Ellie's ears. Or at least, his. Rather than the silky, dulcet tones of the Alurian language, his speech was heavy, guttural.

He's speaking German, she thought. What Alurian speaks German?

He took Leslie's hand and was leading her to the shadows.

"Oh, no. Get away from her, you freak!" Ellie ran to the pair. When she got close, she didn't stop to think. She swung her backpack at the Alurian imposter, smacking him on the head. The man staggered, then with a curse that sounded absolutely perfect in the German tongue, backhanded Ellie, sending her sprawling to the pavement.

That broke Leslie from her spell. "What? Hey!" She pulled back as the Alurian tried to drag her away. She stomped hard on his foot with her heel. As he cried out in surprise, she kneed him in the groin. His howl went up an octave and he buckled over. She kicked off her heels as she pulled Ellie up. Together they ran.

"Jerk ripped my uniform! What was that all about?" Leslie demanded.

"Don Juan. The devil gave him the ability to shapeshift and speak other languages so he could seduce women."

"What? I thought he was just hot."

"Oh, Leslie! Did you even *see* the opera?"

* * *

In the West quadrant, Commander Smythe, having heard Ellie's theory, was contenting himself with using his sonic screwdriver to open doors and start small devices he saw on his way back to the plaza. He'd seen enough Dr. Who to know he really didn't want to wish for anything more until they had a better handle on how real these wishes were.

In the Southern quadrant, Enigo's foes had also taken to the rooftops and were leading him on a wild chase full of dangerous jumps, some gunfire and not a little slipping on roof tiles.

To the East, the city had quickly given way to manicured gardens and fields of vegetables. Botanist Lieutenant Misha Rosien was happily cataloging what she found while Gel kept guard and half-studied for his promotion test. Rosien occasionally asked him a question she remembered from her test. Neither made any wishes nor thought about anything beyond their jobs, thus missing out on all the excitement.

In the Northern quadrant, LeRoy kept running.

In the third-story suite where Enigo had left her, Loreli had settled herself on the chaise lounge and concentrated on retracting the branching growths that had so easily extended to take in the rich soil. She chided herself for letting her guard down so easily. Wasn't this exactly the kind of thing that got her in trouble in the past? But it had felt so good to let go, for just a moment, and give in to her instincts.

A few minutes later, her feet had returned, if not to optimal sexiness, then at least to something functional enough for running with humanoid legs. Enigo had not yet returned. She walked to the balcony. Looking down gave her an intense vertigo that even years of training could not dispel. Looking up didn't help much, either. The street was empty, and she didn't hear anything

200   Karina Fabian

from above. That gave her a sick feeling as well, but she leaned back against the iron railing to look up.

"Enigo?" she called out, but there was no reply. She called again, louder. Tapping her comm badge only produced static. As an experiment, she pulled out her phaser and aimed it at the neighboring building. Nothing.

She shut her eyes, caught between anger and panic. *He wouldn't have left me without good reason. He'll be back. In the meantime, I should find a weapon and shoes. I'll need them, regardless.*

She pushed off the railing and heard a rip. Her uniform had caught on a rough spot in the iron and ripped in the seat. *Wonderful. Now I need a new outfit as well or else I'll have to hide until I can grow something more concealing.*

Mood worsening by the minute, she moved with her hands clasped casually over the tear back into the room. She pulled open the doors of the large wardrobe that dominated one wall, and her mood brightened when she saw the large selection of tasteful and practical safari-style clothing. At least one thing was going her way.

Dressed in full-sear breeches, high boots that were surprisingly comfortable, and a white blouse that tied at the waist and was just a tad too tight around the bosom, Loreli made a methodical search of the drawers for anything she could use as weapons. With each drawer and closet that revealed nothing but fashions and curios, her frustration grew.

"Come on! Enigo needs a weapon and voila! It's the first thing I find. I need one, and there's nothing on the whole floor?" It had been at least half an hour since Enigo had left. She'd heard groaning outside and what she thought was a scream. There had been other sounds, too, that she didn't recognize. More and more, she dreaded venturing outside the relative safety of the house, but she was equally afraid of being trapped there alone.

Downstairs. We found the gun downstairs. That's probably where others will be. Steeling herself against the fear of going to the ground floor unarmed, she stepped onto the first stair.

The front door began to shake.

Loreli grabbed a heavy sculpture of a cupid from the hall table and got ready to throw it at whatever broke through the door.

Instead, the deadbolt, then the knob, turned, and Ellie and Leslie dashed through. They slammed the door quickly and relocked the deadbolt, then leaned against it, panting.

"Up here!" Loreli called, and with a cry of joy, the two ran up the steps even as she ran down. They met on the second-floor landing and embraced. Then Loreli pulled back and examined them with concern. "What happened? You're scratched and your uniforms are torn. Did the zombies get you?"

"Zombies! I thought the LT was putting us on," Leslie babbled, "But they're real and gross and so much faster than anything dead should be!"

"Really gross," Ellie affirmed. "Really fast."

"Did they scratch you?" Loreli demanded again.

"What? No, no these are from the Don Juan." Leslie said.

"And the fall," Ellie added.

"And the chickens. Big chickens."

"Mean chickens."

As if summoned by their conversation, they heard a pecking on the door and a deep bass *bwak*.

They scrambled back up the stairs to the suite and shut the door. Leslie immediately sat on the chaise lounge with a groan. "My feet! I'm sorry, Ellie. I should have listened to you."

"Where are your shoes?" Loreli asked.

"In a backpack, which I threw at a monster chicken. Long story."

Ellie had gone to the washroom and returned with wet towels and wrappings. While she tended Ensign Straus's feet, she gave the Loreli a summary of their adventure, which is left to the reader's imagination except to note that a couple of zombies were mysteriously shot from above, and our heroines managed to escape because some guy in a fez led the angry chicken flock into the zombie horde that was chasing them. "When I looked back, there were feathers and body parts being flung all over."

Leslie added, "And something led us to this building, and the door was locked, but the guy pointed this contraption at it and the door opened. Where'd he go, anyway?"

"Who cares? He's probably imaginary like everything else." Ellie taped the last of the bandage and sat back. "What do we do now? Our communicators stopped working sometime after we started running. Phasers, too."

"We found a weapon downstairs," Loreli said. "I think we should search there and then try to make it to the plaza."

"The pecking stopped, but that doesn't mean the monster chicken has moved on. I think we should wait a bit. Let me look at the communicators. Maybe I can figure out what's wrong with them."

"Good idea. I could use a few minutes to recover," Straus said, "and a new outfit."

For the first time in an hour, Loreli smiled. "That, I can help with."

* * *

You're welcome, Enigo thought at his crewmates as they ran from the mob, which was temporarily distracted by the fact that he'd just shot two of their pack. It wouldn't take long before they realized the fallen weren't getting back up. Shotgun blasts to the head had that effect. Still, it bought them some time.

And him. He took aim at the nearest zombie. His finger eased on the trigger.

A bullet pinged off the stucco beside him.

"Shit!" he rolled away, firing blindly toward his attacker. He was rewarded by a human scream and a plop. Another of Solero's goons gone. But where was that fracking Crip, anyway? It wasn't like him to let others do his dirty work.

Or was it? Hadn't Solero, as Enigo got older and more fearsome, sent others ahead to soften him up before going in for the final blow? Why hadn't he remembered that until now? All this time, he'd painted Solero as someone always bigger and better, but really...

"Ha! You're a coward, Solero! You got weak and yellow, and now I'm coming after you!"

* * *

In the distance, Smythe thought he heard the distinct *VWORP VWORP* of a time machine with the emergency brake on. He looked toward the north, momentarily tempted, then decided, no, he had to get back to the plaza and connect with his own companions first.

With his realization giving him fresh motivation, Enigo was able to pick off the last of the Crips and was in hot pursuit of Solero and Barbie. He'd even managed to nudge them back toward the building where Loreli was holed up and toward which he'd seen Doall and Straus run. With any luck, they'd have found weapons and he could draft his ensign into the chase while Doall and Loreli made their way to the plaza. He'd decided to capture Solero and his bae and drag them back to Smythe. If anyone on this planet had the answers they needed, it was them. Maybe he'd even let Solero live afterward, if the Crip was sufficiently humiliated.

He loved his job.

Toward the East, Gel and Rosien took a slightly different path back to the plaza and found themselves taking a longer, more roundabout route. When Rosien complained about the long walk, they turned a corner and found a lot of vehicles bearing the sign "Please Enjoy!" Of course, there was one that fit all of Gel's automotive dreams.

LeRoy kept running. He dashed into a boarded-up store and leaned against the door panting for two beats, then checked his phaser again. Useless! If only he had… He looked up and realized he'd stepped into a tack and feed store. There were farm implements, bridles, chicken feed.

Minutes later, a five-foot hen patrolling the area in front of the store and occasionally scratching for a tidbit squawked in surprise when the door burst open, disgorging a HuFleet redshirt, armed with a scythe and rope, a bridle hanging off his shoulder. The redshirt let out a rebel yell. The hen squawked again and ran, Jenkins in hot pursuit. A small bag of feed bounced off his hip.

"LeeeRoy Jenkins!"

* * *

In fact, a thorough search of the house did not turn up weapons except for some dull kitchen knives, but Ellie did find a set of archaic watchmaker's tools like her eccentric uncle used to have. The trio retired to the suite where the two ensigns changed into different clothes from the safari collection. Ellie found a tan split skirt, tall boots and olive-green safari shirt with puff sleeves and a peplum bottom, tied with a wide belt. It was exactly what Barbie used to wear on episodes that took her to jungle planets. Leslie found khaki shorts with a white V-neck T-shirt. Her phaser belt was loose over the tee, and she added a whip to the ensemble, the closest thing to a weapon she could find, though it was too short and the braided leather too soft to effectively injure anyone. Hiking boots with high socks covered her bandages.

Ellie took apart a phaser, a tricorder, and her communicator and was trying to kludge together something that would let them reach the ship, or at least the First Officer.

Straus, in the meantime, had searched the wardrobes until she found a slinky green dress and yellow tights. These, she ripped into pieces, knotting three strips of yellow into a long piece of the gown. She did this three times, then tied a piece of her work to each of the four windows, with an extra piece at the balcony of their own suite.

"There! Now anyone passing by will know the three of us are here and trapped."

"I'm worried about Enigo," Loreli said from where Leslie had set her to sharpening the knives. "Perhaps you should arm yourself and find him?"

"And leave two bridge officers alone and unarmed? Ha! This is my first away mission on the Impulsive, and I'd like to have another. We go together, or we call for rescue."

Suddenly, the door opened and Enigo stepped through. The ladies all jumped.

"Sir! We didn't hear you."

"Yeah, 'cause I'm stealthy like a jungle cat," he smirked at them in a confident, almost come-on way. Then his gaze settled on Loreli. "Give me a minute alone with Loreli, all right?"

"Why?" Doall asked.

"None of your business. Leslie, take the Ensign and head back to the rendezvous point now. We'll catch up."

"Sir, we're unarmed. The zombies."

"Are taken care of. Now go!" His eyes flared in a way that brooked no argument. Ellie scooped her half-done project into her backpack and they headed out the door.

Loreli looked with confusion from the door Enigo closed behind the two officers to his steamy stare. "Enigo, what could you possibly need to talk to me about right now?"

"Something I should have said to you a long time ago," he stepped toward her, and the smolder in his expression made her step back.

"Enigo, are you all right?"

"I could be, with your help."

* * *

On the landing, Straus said, "That was weird. Did he call me 'Leslie'?"

"He was raised on the Hood," Ellie said. "What does he know about jungle cats? Oh, no! Turn off your translator!"

They ran back to the bedroom suite and pressed their ears against the door. Rather than human speech, however, they head the swishing and whooshing of the Botanical language. They looked at each other in horror.

"Don Juan!"

The door was locked and no man with a whirry tube-thingy was there to open it. They began to pound on the wood. "Loreli! It's not Enigo!"

* * *

Their warnings were not heard through the thick door, but no one needed to tell Loreli something was wrong. As she backed toward the open balcony, she snatched one of the knives from the table. Enigo just laughed.

"Got a little spunk in you, hm? I can play rough."

"Enigo, something is wrong. Think. Did you ingest something? Maybe stop to smell an exotic flower that sprayed you with mood-altering pollen?"

"Yours is the only scent I desire." He stepped closer, uncaring of the blade she held or too confident that she would not use it.

* * *

Enigo crouched behind a chimney of the building just across from the house where he'd left Loreli. A quick glance at the balcony had shown him Straus' signal. Smart one, that Ensign. She might become a recurring character yet. But Solero and Barbie had stopped just two roofs over. It looked like Barbie had broken a strap and when Solero tried to help her, it turned into a make-out session. Did that mean he had time to get reinforcements or that he should act fast before they'd had enough or got really messy?

He glanced back at the balcony, thinking to signal his crewmates, and saw Loreli, dressed in tight pants, backed against the railing and pointing a knife at...himself?

Thoughts of Solero and Vixen Barbie fled his mind. He aimed the shotgun, then thought better. The spray was too wide. This wasn't like stunning both hostage and hostage-taker. His phaser was still set to grappling gun. He ran across the roof and leaped, shooting the gun at the same time and trusting it to find purchase.

No one attacked his Ship's Sexy!

* * *

It must be an aphrodisiac, Loreli thought as she bumped against the railing. A strong one at that. He's completely lost his wits!

"Enigo, please. Concentrate. I need you to clear your head. How about a cold shower?"

"Will you join me? Come on. There's really no need for a knife, is there?"

She should slice him. It might wake him up, but she couldn't. Even if he forgave her later, she couldn't.

He eased the knife out of her hand. "Better."

He leaned closer. She felt her fronts stand on end as they prepared their defense. "Enigo, please, don't..."

Space Traipse: Hold My Beer, Season 1 ﹡ 211

Suddenly something shoved her and Enigo from behind. Enigo was catapulted into the room, but she staggered and fell into the arms of...

"Enigo?" But this Enigo was sweaty and sooty, his uniform sleeve torn from a glancing blow of some kind of projectile weapon. He was grinning his excited, half-feral grin he had in battle, a familiar and comforting sight.

"Now, this ups my morale!" he declared.

She wanted to laugh, but she was too confused. "But, what? How?"

"Next time someone comes on to you like that and you have the chance, cut them. I don't care who it is," he scolded.

She saw the faux Enigo rise up and grab the knife. "Behind you!"

He flung her out of the way in a move that was almost dance-like and brought the shotgun up just in time to block his other self's blow. Then he twisted and smashed the butt into his other self's back. FauxEnigo staggered, wiped his lip and growled. He ran at Enigo, an amateur move. The Chief of Security stepped aside and ducked low, using the barrel of the rifle to sweep the other man off his feet and over the balcony, then he hefted the gun into position and shot his attacker on the way down.

FauxEnigo hit the ground with a sloppy *thunk*.

Enigo ran to the balcony, balancing on the bars to better aim over the side. When his opponent didn't move, he let out a trilling cry of his old gang. "*Damstrate!* The ship is family – and no one messes with my family!"

From the roof, someone yelled, "Yo, Blood!"

Enigo looked up and to the left

Solero shot him three times in the chest.

Enigo let out one curse, then fell off the balcony.

Loreli screamed.

* * *

Smythe had just made it to the plaza when he heard Loreli's scream. He took off in the direction from which it came.

The suite door suddenly gave way, and the two ladies ran to the balcony where they saw Loreli leaning over the railing and sobbing. Ellie also screamed, but Leslie grabbed them both and pulled them into the room. She ducked into the bathroom and retrieved the first aid kit Ellie had found and the three dashed down the stairs.

Rosien and Gel decided that even in a car, the scenic route was not the best decision, after all, and retraced their steps to find the wide avenue they'd originally used.

LeRoy kept running, but once again, he was the pursuer. He liked it better that way.

* * *

The first aid kit was a useless gesture. Enigo was dead.

Now of course, anyone who has read the blog or watched ST:TOS "Shore Leave" knows Enigo isn't really dead, but for the sake of the story, suspend what you know and let yourself get immersed in the scene:

Loreli kneeling at the body, no longer screaming but in shocked grief. Tears run down her perfect face, not blotching her complexion at all. Her hands hover over his arm, his chest, his face, as if afraid to touch him. She bites back a delicate sob.

Ellie muttering denials as she checks his wrist, his neck, her tricorder, for any sign of life. Straus standing, dumbstruck, and thinking, "This is my fault. If I hadn't imagined Don Juan, he wouldn't have gone after Loreli and the LT wouldn't have been on the balcony at that moment. It's my fault. Oh, gods, this is not how I want to get bridge duty."

Smythe thunders up the alley, slowing as he sees the bodies. Ellie looks up, cheeks tear-streaked and blotchy, and shakes her head. In the background, sad, tense music plays. Smyth crouches in front of the body. He presses a hand against his lips in an expression of guilt and grief. Since the captain wasn't there, it was his job to emote the regret and self-blame of a commander losing a redshirt, after all.

Suddenly, Straus broke the iconic scene. "Sir!"

Solero and Barbie dropped from the rooftop. Solero raised his gun and Barbie lifted her ninja sword with a loud kia (the ninja war cry, not the car).

Smythe pointed his sonic screwdriver at them, and the two toppled.

As Straus cautiously approached the bodies, knife out and whip ready, Ellie and Loreli went to the First Officer. "How did you know that would work?" Doall asked.

"I didn't. I simply wished it would."

"And that's exactly the point!" a stranger's voice said from a convenient alcove. They turned to find a humanoid male in forest green velour robes with gold filigree, a daring fashion choice favored by too many unknown alien species. When the Impulsive crew turned weapons on him, he held up his hands in peaceable surrender. "Oh, that won't be necessary. You see, we're just realizing you don't have a complete understanding of how this world works."

"You take our wishes and innermost desires and somehow manufacture situations to make them reality," Smythe said, because as ranking officer, he got to take credit for the thought work his people did. RHIP.

The man sputtered, his prepared speech apparently derailed. "Well, yes, but you don't understand the limits. This is meant solely for your entertainment, and—"

"Entertainment? Limits? Your constructs shot my LT!" Straus yelled. She flung her hand back to point at the body, but it, FauxEnigo, and the two gang members were gone.

"What did you do with my LT?" She launched herself at the man, but Smythe caught her before she could bury her knife into his chest.

"Please calm down, and I'll explain. You see, this is exactly what I'm talking about. We weren't prepared for the more extreme and on occasion, dark, desires of your subconscious."

"Like Don Juan?" Ellie asked.

"Hey! I just thought he was some hot romantic guy, maybe a little...extreme...in his appetites. I didn't want someone all slimy and rapey."

"Of course not, but this is where conflicting desires came into play. Ensign Doall knew what the legendary Don Juan was really supposed to be like, and she also has a strong need to be right in all situations."

"So, it's my fault he's all slimy and rapey?" Ellie exclaimed. "*I'm* the reason Enigo got killed?"

From behind them, a familiar voice said, "*Vero*! And if I had really died, I'd be pissed."

Enigo stood before them, whole, clean, and wearing a Kevlar vest and multiple projectile weapons, bandoliers and a couple of grenades over his uniform. Hanging on his arm was Barbie, dressed in tight leathers

216   ✿   Karina Fabian

and loose weaponry and staring at him with a besotted smile.

"Enigo!" Ellie ran to him and hugged him. Then she stepped back and smacked him on the arm. "How could you scare us like that?"

The other ladies had similar urges, of course, but Enigo was Straus' superior officer, and Loreli, even in the throes of grief, was too much a professional to show such blatant favoritism. She would find a quieter time to tell him of her great relief.

He gaped at her, then laughed. "It wasn't my idea. I thought I'd legit bought it. Damn, that hurt, then everything went black, and then I woke up and was totally healed. Except for the scars. I kept those."

"The scars are amazing," Barbie oozed, caressing his chest over the Kevlar.

"And the young lady?" Smythe asked.

"Oh, right! Sir, meet Barbie Fifty-Seven. Time runs differently underground. I was all healed and making my way up when I heard flamenco music coming out of this little cantina, and there they were. Dance halls are neutral territory on the Hood, so I went in for a drink and, well."

"Solero is good in a fight," Barbie concluded, "but when it comes to dancing, he's got nothing on Enigo."

"I'm suave like a jungle cat, right Vixen?"

Barbie made a playful growl in reply.

"So you see," the alien caretaker said in conclusion. "Everything turned out all right in the end, and we're recalibrating our systems to better account for the wilder variations of the human mind. In fact, with a brief orientation, there should be less confusion."

"Confusion?" Smythe cocked a brow derisively. "Resuscitated or not, a valued member of my crew was killed."

Enigo jumped to the caretaker's defense. "Well, yeah. I shot zombies, did a heroic rescue, died a romantically tragic death... Plus, I stole my rival's bae. All in what, a couple of hours? Best shore leave ever!"

If the members of the away team thought they were done gaping for the day, they were mistaken. They all stared at Enigo, jaws dropped.

"The only thing left on my wish list is payback on that Solero for killin' me. Please, sir? Can I stay a little longer?"

A roar of an engine interrupted their discussion, and a ZAT (Zombie Apocalypse Truck, for those that have forgotten the mention in Episode One) trundled up the alley. A long, thick pseudopod bearing Gel's head stuck itself out the driver's side window. "Here you are! Look what I found. And the controls are all made for Globbals. Can you believe it?"

Rosien jumped out of the passenger side and took in the Chief of Security and his impossibly proportioned apocalyptic eye candy. "Did we miss something?"

Ellie pulled her aside to explain while Enigo and Barbie went to admire Gel's vehicle and discuss the weaponry.

Smythe took the moment to approach the unusually quiet Loreli. "Are you all right, Lieutenant?"

She nodded, but her skin was paler than usual. "I will be. This has not been what I'd consider fun."

She cast the caretaker one of the darkest looks Smythe had ever seen from her.

The caretaker gave her a sad smile and a bow. "My apologies, my dear. We were addressing your primary desire to improve the morale of Lieutenant LaFuentes."

"That's so you!" Barbie cooed.

The caretaker continued. "But perhaps now we can find something more suited to your needs?"

This seemed to mollify the Botanical, but Smythe addressed the Caretaker sternly. "I'll want certain guarantees in place. When it comes to death and injury, Lieutenant LaFuentes's race is especially psychologically hardy, but I will not have my crew dealing with PTSD from a shore leave excursion."

"Of course, of course. Shall we discuss this with your captain?"

A low *bwak!* echoed off the stone walls of the building. Everyone went alert. Even Barbie drew a nine mil from her holster.

A seven-foot Calusian Brown rounded the corner, a triumphant LeRoy Jenkins riding its back, reins in hand.

"LeRoy!" Straus exclaimed. "You did it!"

"Yeah!" LeRoy hopped off the bird and walked it to the gathering security team. "I caught this monster chicken and made her my hen. Yaaaaa!"

"Yaaaaa!" the redshirts shouted back.

"Yaaaaa! Then I'm going back and making her demon brood my dinner. Yaaaaa!"

"Yaaaaa! Bar-be-que!"

In a rare display of emotion, Smythe pinched the bridge of his nose. "Perhaps we should get to discussing limits with my Captain. Unfortunately, our comms are inoperative."

"Yes, unfortunately, that was part of LaFuentes' fantasy. He has an unusually strong will. We've had to recalibrate our systems twice to compensate. They should be fine, now. But please, let's discuss this in more hospitable surroundings."

"Sir?" Enigo said. "Solero is still out there, and by now, he's regathering his gang…"

Smythe waved one hand indulgently. "All right, Lieutenant, but some restraint, please? Not all wishes should be granted."

"*No problemo*! Who wants to kick zombie and Crip butt?" he asked the group at large.

LeRoy answered by mounting his fowl and shouting his own name. Gel revved his engines.

"Could I just go shopping?" Rosien asked timidly.

Straus smiled. "You know, I think my tastes for danger run a different way."

"Do they?" A suave dapper man leaned stylishly against a wall. He wore a gray suit and an even grayer tie. "I'd like to hear more."

Leslie smiled and sauntered toward him. "Perhaps over lunch?"

"I think that could be arranged." He slid his hand around her waist. His grip tightened lightly on her whip as they strolled away.

Enigo rolled his eyes. "Loreli? Doall?"

Loreli shook her head. "I think I'd prefer to join the commander and learn more about these people."

"Of course." The caretaker waved his hand down the alley. "This way."

From a blue box a few feet ahead of them, a tall man with a red fez and a facial tattoo said, "Oi, Smythe, maybe when you're done with the caretaker, you'll have time for an adventure in time and space?"

Inside, Smythe's inner child squealed and did a little dance, but aloud he said, "Of course – but an adventure in time, please. I have adventures in space every day."

It was a line he'd practiced in his mind since he was a plebe at the Academy, and he was thrilled to find it rolled off his tongue with such droll casualness. But when the Doctor tossed him the key to the TARDIS, he almost lost his composure.

"Just make a wish," Doctor 34 said, then stepped into his blue police box. With a *VWORP VWORP*, which according to the comics is the official way to write the TARDIS sound — don't blame me — he and the box disappeared.

Smythe cleared his throat and indicated for the caretaker to continue on.

That left only Ellie standing alone, backpack still on her shoulder, uncertain what to do next.

"Well, Doall?" LaFuentes said to her. He jerked his head at the ZAT, and Gel revved the engine invitingly.

"Me?" Doall blinked. "I dunno. I'm not really a fighter…"

"Come on!" Ninja astrophysicist flamenco dancer Barbie cajoled. "I believe in you!"

"Yeah. Just don't wish me dead again, and we'll be fine."

"Well, okay." As she clambered in next to the squealing and clapping Barbie, she asked Enigo, "What do you know about jungle cats?"

"Ai, *chica*, we had National Geographic in our library."

"Strong, suave and smart, too. Isn't he just wikadas?" Barbie sighed, then said, "Ooo! I love your outfit!"

Gel hit the gas, and they tore down the cobbled streets, a man on a chicken racing along behind.

"LeRoy Jenkins!"

* * *

Captain's Log, Supplemental

After some cordial discussions and the creation of a brief training video, Commander Smythe and I feel comfortable allowing our crew to make use of the shore leave planet. The Caretakers, as we've dubbed them, are really a remarkable people. A species of pure thought who inhabit the vastness of the nebula, they are nonetheless aware of the corporeal creatures that traverse it at a much slower pace. Out of kindness and sheer neighborliness, they took it upon themselves to create this rest stop and take great delight in watching us play. We've taxed their systems a bit – LaFuentes, in particular – so we decided to allow the current team to remain and complete their leave time in order to "work out the kinks." In the meantime, the medical and mental health teams have set up a rotation, taking into account stress levels and varying interests in order to make it easier for the Caretakers to accommodate us without too much trouble.

Space Traipse: Hold My Beer, Season 1 ❦ 223

I'm heading down to Teleporter Room one to meet the party as they return to get a first-hand report before I head out myself.

Captain Tiberius wore a flannel shirt and waders and held a pole in one hand and tackle in the other. His floppy hat had a variety of flies stuck in it along with a pin of a fish jumping out of a map of Texas. The Teleporter Chief gave his captain a single cursory glance before deciding the better part of valor was to tend to his equipment.

"My mistress sees our comrades and desires their destruction and rebirth," he intoned.

If that sounded odd to the captain, then he, too, chose the better part and ignored it. "By all means, zap them up."

A moment later, the away team appeared on the teleporter pad. Ensign Rosien, dressed in a flaring skirt and white heels, her hair perfectly coifed and make-up immaculate, picked up her bags and strutted to the teleporter console. She handed Chief Dour two slips of paper.

"The items at these coordinates need to be 'ported to the botany lab. The boxes at these should go straight to my room. Thank you!" She gave the captain a smart nod and strode out.

Lieutenant LaFuentes looked ragged, dirty, bloody, and absolutely elated. He had a rose tucked behind his ear.

"Best shore leave ever, sir!" he hooted as he all but bounced off the pad. Minion Gel O'Tin followed behind, less energetic and a little splotchy, but also seemingly content. Ensign Jenkins, too, seemed bedraggled but pleased; he wore a necklace of chicken bones and was still sucking on a drumstick.

Ensign Doall dragged herself behind them. Her hair was a mess despite it being tied into a tight ponytail. She, too, was smudged with dirt and blood, and a bruise darkened her cheek.

"It was...interesting," Doall offered. "It certainly stretched my horizons."

"Doall held her own, Captain. Not bad for an ops officer," LaFuentes said.

Doall gave him a look that was at once proud, weary and *What-the-hell-was-I-thinking*? "Yes, sir. Thank you, sir. Request permission to go to Sickbay?"

Jeb gave her an understanding smile. It took a special kind of crazy to volunteer for one of LaFuentes' training exercises. He could hardly imagine the real deal. "Granted."

"Thank you, sir." She made her slow way from the room. He thought he heard her say something about her childhood being ruined.

Space Traipse: Hold My Beer, Season 1 ❧ 225

"How about you, Straus?" Enigo asked. "Enjoy yourself?"

Straus was again in her mended uniform, but there was nothing regulation about the dreamy smile on her face. "Oh, my horizons were stretched as well. With your permission, sir? Ellie! Wait up!"

Smythe was next off the pad, having delayed to rearrange the crown of gold leaves on his head and make sure his toga didn't reveal anything, as well as to give the other characters a chance to get their lines in. "Nova of a time, Captain. Simply brilliant!" he said.

"Maybe you should change into uniform before reporting to the bridge?" Jeb suggested.

"Right. Fantastic time, sir. I'm sure you'll enjoy it."

"How about you, Loreli?" Enigo asked the last person to walk off the teleporter pad. "You missed all the fun."

Like Straus, Loreli had returned to her standard uniform, including issue shoes. Her demeanor and color had also returned to normal, which Jeb was glad to see.

"Hardly, Enigo. I had some fascinating conversations with the Caretakers, and they were kind enough to show me their true form and give me some insight into their lives as pure thought. It will make a fascinating paper."

Enigo shrugged. "Well, when you finish that paper, see me. I think you need a few more lessons in self-defense. You can't depend on those frond spikes of yours to get you out of every situation."

"Later," Jeb told her. "What you just did, Lieutenant, is called 'work,' so you'll be walking those feet back down to the planet and rooting them into some rich, planetborn soil. The Caretakers told me about this lovely quiet stream. Gentle breezes, lots of fish."

She almost seemed to bloom at the idea. "I think I'd enjoy that very much, Captain."

"Shall we, then?" He hefted his rod and tackle in one hand and offered her his other arm.

We close this story with a peaceful scene of a fisherman in a stream. Thigh-deep in the water, Jeb cast out with lazy sweeps of his hand, not really caring if he caught anything, but certain he would. It was that kind of planet. On the shore, near where a blooming willow lowered its branches to brush against the gently flowing waters, Loreli stood. Her feet had again grown, reaching into the ground and peeking out to be caressed by the stream. Her fronds were splayed, and she held out her arms gracefully to take in the sun, the breeze, the gently blowing pollen. Everything.

It was good.

I sent my love to space today
Atomized to a quantum spray
Her deepest self reduced to cold equations.
One miscalculation
And she loved me no more.

Enjoyed the book? Help keep more adventures coming.

Join my Patreon. Support my writing (and those whose work go to the production of my books) and get advanced episodes, character interviews, redshirt opportunities and more.

https://www.patreon.com/KarinaFabian

Thanks for Reading!

Back in 2016, I was tired and stressed and wanted a way to let off some steam and write without putting pressure on myself. Star Trek parody seemed to be just the thing, and thanks to a Tumblr post about how humans are the most feared species because of their lack of impulse control, **Space Traipse: Hold My Beer** was born. It's become a long-running serial on my blog. You can find the stories here with their links: http://karinafabian.com/space-traipse-hold-my-beer/.

I wrote these as humor therapy, so they went straight from my head to the computer screen with only the most cursory of editing. You'll see the typos and CHARACTERNAMEHERE reminders that I somehow still forgot. And, as one person said, they are "One. Installment.

A. Week." That's when I learned folks binge them like Netflix. Therefore, I decided to start compiling them into collections. I also took the time to fix up errors. Speaking of...

I'd like to thank the beta readers who so generously gave their time to seek out my typos: Tamara Wilhite, Deborah Cullins Smith, Kerrie Lapoehn (hey, cuz!), and Annette Tenny. They are awesome friends, and many are awesome writers, too. Thanks, guys – I hope you enjoyed the book.

I have an intermittent newsletter, so if you want to know about my latest works or hear from Vern, my dragon private eye, please subscribe: https://tinyurl.com/fabianspacenews.

I no longer dream of being a best seller, but I still enjoy knowing that my stories are read. Please, if you liked the collection, write a review on Amazon or at least give it some stars. Contact me via my website, comment on my blog or Facebook page, but also, please tell others!

Thanks again for joining me in my travels.

About the Author

Do you have any idea how crowded it gets when a dragon lives in your brain? Add to that nuns in space, psychotic psychics and redneck spacefarers, and you have a pretty good idea why Karina Fabian started writing her stories. She has 16 books to date and is working on more. She's also a founder of the Catholic Writers Guild. She's happily married to Rob, who tolerates her spaciness and adores her imagination and humor (in other words, the perfect husband.) They have four children.